All ey

"Miss Foster, ...ion
Penny wonde... his request won ...me
well-meaning soul would see fit to warn him away.

"Thank you," she said simply. As she gripped the
muscled strength of his arm, she considered what it
might be like to fulfill their wildest assumptions
with this marksman, her Cupid.

All eyes followed their exit from the room as he
plucked up her cloak without having to be told
which one. He swung its warmth about her shoulders, the embrace of the cloak intoxicating, and yet
his hands did not linger. He offered no further reason for gossip.

"Velvet suits you. Begs touching," he said.

A suggestive remark, an unmistakably teasing
glint in his eyes, and yet he made no move to put
words to action, as others would have. Did he lack
desire? Or an awareness of her reputation? Or did
the faces at the fogged window make him keep his
hands to himself?

She took comfort in the woolen warmth and solidity of his arm's support, in his deferent manner,
and yet she did not trust him. . . .

Captain Cupid
Calls the Shots

Elisabeth Fairchild

A SIGNET BOOK

SIGNET
Published by New American Library, a division of
Penguin Putnam Inc., 375 Hudson Street,
New York, New York 10014, U.S.A.
Penguin Books Ltd, 27 Wrights Lane,
London W8 5TZ, England
Penguin Books Australia Ltd, Ringwood,
Victoria, Australia
Penguin Books Canada Ltd, 10 Alcorn Avenue,
Toronto, Ontario, Canada M4V 3B2
Penguin Books (N.Z.) Ltd, 182–190 Wairau Road,
Auckland 10, New Zealand

Penguin Books Ltd, Registered Offices:
Harmondsworth, Middlesex, England

First published by Signet, an imprint of New American Library,
a division of Penguin Putnam Inc.

First Printing, December 2000
10 9 8 7 6 5 4 3 2 1

PUBLISHER'S NOTE
This is a work of fiction. Names, characters, places, and incidents either
are the product of the author's imagination or are used fictitiously,
and any resemblance to actual persons, living or dead, business establish-
ments, events or locales is entirely coincidental.

Dedicated to
all those whose lives have been clouded
by mistaken assumptions,
and

In memory of
Mary and Henry,
who ran away with the gypsies.

Chapter One

Silvered mist shrouded the vale of Eden. The hills beyond appeared ghostlike and uncertain in the light of the just risen sun.

Beneath him the trees struck counterpoint in dark gray, leafless silhouette, hunchbacked by the wind, ranks of them, standing guard at the edges of every mist-cloaked field. Many a morning he had stood guard, just so—mornings best forgotten.

He rode a length or two ahead of the others into the cold, wet, unfamiliar landscape. Fogged, like his thoughts. It had become his habit to ride a little apart, lost in looking rather than in thought, leaving his companions to what seemed unending conversation, their voices a low murmur at his back, reminding him of all he wanted to forget.

He saw it first, emerging from the mists ahead, the swaying rump of a pony, first gray, the fog's deception, then brown, a liverish color with a gray-brown mane and tail, its gait uneven, a woman leading the animal, nothing gray about her.

She clutched a purple cloak about her slender form, hem held high. The braided straw bonnet glowed golden.

His horse, a towering gray beast that had charged unfaltering into the frey at Waterloo, this faithful, sure-footed creature that had carried him to safety when he had taken a shot in the calf, slipped now in the mud, hooves thumping.

The brown pony snorted, breath pluming, hind legs jacking out to kick assumed danger.

The woman started, her bonnet swiveling, fear large in dark eyes reflecting the cloak's color—amethyst eyes. He saw nothing else for a long, searching moment in which bejeweled eyes questioned the very quality of his being.

Pale lashes veiled her regard. The moment passed. She looked away—left him longing for another glimpse of a troubled soul.

He took in the rest of her. Nested in the deep purple lining of the bonnet, fair wisps of damp curl framed a heart-shaped face. Mist dewed petal-soft skin while cold put blush to each translucent cheek. A fragile flower, she bloomed in these cold, bleak surroundings.

Shy flower, she urged the pony farther out of the road with a cluck of the tongue and a tug on the halter.

Alexander was used to the look of fear in the eyes of the young women of France, of Belgium. But his own countrywoman? What had she to fear in him? Did the weather-worn uniform intimidate her, or his road-wearied condition? Or was it merely that he was a stranger to her, in a place where strangers were few? He slowed his mount to a walk.

"Are you . . ." His voice came out gruff with disuse—the first time he had volunteered speech in two days—the first time he had addressed a decent young Englishwoman since his return. He cleared his throat and tried again. "Beg pardon, miss, are you in need of assistance? Has the pony gone lame?"

The back of her bonnet shook a vigorous no. On she plodded, shoulders hunched, as if to make herself smaller in his eyes.

Was it his appearance that frightened her? Had he shaved this morning? He stroked his chin, relieved to discover it smooth. He had neglected such niceties of late—since their return. Val had rousted them early every morning, pushed them to the limits of exhaustion every evening. "C'mon, lads," he would remind them, even when he staggered drunkenly to the saddle and they both feared he must fall from the horse. "Must make it home in time for m'birthday. Sleep all you like once we're there."

And here they were, on Valentine's Day, the distance almost covered.

Val shouted from behind him. "Who've you found, Cupid? Piercing local hearts already, are you?"

The young woman turned, eyes wide, sparkling with an intensity of emotion.

"Val!" she murmured, the name thick in her throat. And then, face shuttered by the brim of the bonnet, she turned her back on them, cloak whirling. With a chirrup to the pony, she walked on.

Val and Oscar rode abreast, Val taking a quick pull from the hip flask he always carried.

"Offended her, have you?" he jested, eyes bright with the spirits, attention fixed on the girl, recognition there, and was it contempt?

Alexander opened his mouth on objection, but Val winked and said, "Never mind. Touch-me-not is easily offended."

"Touch me what?"

Val did not wait to explain. He rode after the girl—always did—with no more luck than Alexander this time. She would not turn her face to him, though he leaned down in the saddle to speak. The brisk shake of her head was unmistakable. In fact, every line of her body spoke of rejection.

Touch me not, Alexander thought.

Beside him, Oscar said quietly, "Looks as if our lad has lost his touch."

Alexander nodded as he watched the girl strike off again with a resolution that inspired admiration. In her steadfast refusals, in the straight-backed sway of the cloak at her heels, he found a pleasing level of independence and self-sufficiency.

"Come, lads!" Val beckoned, and turning his horse rode past the young woman with a flick of his quirt and a show of his horse's heels.

They trotted after him, tipping hats to the young woman. She did not so much as acknowledge them with a nod. When Alexander turned his head in hopes of one last look into her eyes, she wore an expression of proud reserve, her gaze distant, even unfriendly.

Well out of earshot of the woman, Val announced, "And so you meet the flower of Appleby, who is both the most and least hospitable of all the blossoms hereabouts. Miss Touch-me-not herself."

"Why insult her?" Alexander asked.

"Insult her?" Val laughed harshly. "Nonsense. She has been just such an oddity since she was a girl: remote, unapproachable, socially inept. She generally has more use for animals than for people. Tames wild ponies, straight off the fells, and as wild as her horseflesh in her own way. She is constantly shadowed by a man-eating dog. I wonder where he is today."

"How unlike you, Val, to speak ill of a female," Alexander persisted.

Val reached for his hip flask, wrenched off the cap, and met Alexander's gaze with the same intensity with which he had met the French. "Is it?" he asked.

The strength of his words surprised Alexander. For an instant his comrade in arms seemed a stranger as he threw back his handsome head and downed another mouthful.

"Has our Val been spurned by the girl or bitten by the man-eater?" Oscar dared ask, one brow raised, gray eyes inquisitive.

"Ha! They are one and the same," Val snapped, screwing the lid back onto the flask, the tension of the moment broken, the cheeky grin he gave them all too familiar. He spurred his mount into startled motion.

"Should have held my tongue," Oscar chastised himself, tweaking at his mustache, as he always did when he was nervous. He had tweaked it almost into oblivion in the greatest furor of fighting. "Lad's in one of his moods," he said. "This homecoming, perhaps."

"And you?" Alexander asked. "Have you no homecoming to look forward to?"

Oscar smoothed thinning hair away from an intelligent brow and frowned. "I find myself strangely reluctant." The frown melted into a lopsided grin beneath the sketchy mustache. "Curious, isn't it?"

Alexander thought of his own postponed homecoming as he gigged the gray into motion. "Not in the least."

Nerves on edge, spine stiff, her breath rasping too loud in her own ears, clouding the air before her, she watched them ride into the mists that led to Appleby, three young men in the dark green-and-black velvet uniform of the 95th, the turned-back blacks of their coattails bobbing in rhythm with their horses' gaits, black tassels swaying, cockaded shakos a bit bedraggled in the mist.

Nut brown of complexion, fine of figure, backs straight and tall, legs lean and muscular, the war had shaped them, hardened them. They wore a hungry keenness in their eyes—a dangerous keenness.

Brisk, brash, beloved Valentine Wharton had come home. *Alive!* His mother would be pleased, as would be the mothers of suitable unmarried daughters throughout the county. She wondered if they would notice, or even care, that something had changed in his eyes—some former lighthearted, self-confident brightness was now subdued.

He had smelled of strong spirits, just like the last time she had seen him. "Lady Anne, Lady Anne," she whispered, "give me strength."

She closed her eyes, remembering that day.

He had spoken kindly, as kindly as in meeting her today. She had almost forgotten that quality in his voice. *Deceitful sound.* How it made her heart betray her better sense. How could it race, after the way he had left her?

As for his companions, the quiet, slender fellow looked like a ferret—wily creature.

The other—Cupid. She guessed him a rogue. Why else call a man Cupid? And he the first man she had seen today, Valentine's Day, which meant, if one believed the old superstition, that they must marry. She could not restrain a sharp, short laugh.

Small chance of that.

Cupid—unlike any rococo cupid she had ever seen depicted. Nothing cherubic about him. Tall, lean, broad-shouldered. Muscled thighs gripped the saddle, muscled hands the reins. Low-voiced, this cupid, with a peculiarly rigid jaw, as if he refrained too often from speaking his mind.

No cupid curls. He had dark hair—cropped short—straight as broom bristle, and keen eyes, bright as glass, green like the cockade that topped his shako.

No mischief in those eyes as he had offered assistance. She had expected mischief from a friend of Val's. But there had been only curiosity there—concern, surprise, and something darker, guardedly wistful—not at all what she thought of in connection with Valentine, or a cupid.

What struck her most about him was the largeness of him—not size, though both he and the gray were big—no, it was more a sense of how he filled the space around him. He seemed somehow to overflow the boundaries of his muscular form, to change the very air.

Not she. She was the mist that swirled and eddied in his wake.

Foolish thought. She trudged on, cheeks and fingertips cold, the core of her body heated by her exertions, by her encounter.

"Lady Anne, Lady Anne," she said aloud. The pony's ear swiveled. "Why should I be the first to see Valentine! Riding into Appleby on Valentine's Day, of all days! And with him, a cupid." She laughed, the rich sound of her own amusement too loud in the stillness. The pony lifted his head with a snort.

She stroked the velvet softness of his nose with gloved hand and pressed her cheek to his strongly boned head. "Ah, Archer, lad, Lady Anne gives me no answer."

Archer's clipped ears flicked forward, listening. The depths of his brown eyes seemed to understand her every word.

Ahead, the fog swallowed the uniformed men, leaving her alone with the wet clop of hooves, the sound of her own breath, and the wet drip of the trees.

She had learned to enjoy the stillness, felt safer there, none but Archer to keep her silent company, the two of them wrapped in the receding walls of fog. A familiar state of being.

Familiar too, the faint regret, the inner doubt. It matched what she had seen in Cupid's eyes. Perhaps she should have said yes, allowed him to help her. Who better suited, after all, on Valentine's Day?

Chapter Two

They trotted across a small, mist-draped sandstone bridge, the River Eden chuckling beneath, winter-stripped trees standing attention along its banks. As they pushed their tired mounts up a gently rising street, Val pointed out the looming castle keep.

"Caesar's Tower. Norman Conquest," he said.

They clopped past a tall pillar, street lamp at the base, weather vane at the top, marking the main cross street. It bore the motto, RETAIN YOUR LOYALTY, PRESERVE YOUR RIGHTS.

"Lady Anne," he explained.

They stared at him blankly.

"Countess of Dorset, Pembroke and Montgomery. Surely you've heard of her?"

His fair brows rose when they shook their heads.

"Opposed Cromwell. Had a hand in rebuilding almost every church and castle in the district. These almshouses are her doing." He waved at the red stone buildings they approached. "She's quite the thing around here."

Alexander cared nothing of this Lady Anne. His thoughts still centered on the young woman, the sweet shape of her face, the unusual color of her eyes. Why did Val bristle so in her company? Why declare her a touch-me-not? Unless, of course, he had been rebuffed in the touching of her.

Ahead of them a black-and-white building intruded upon the avenue, Moot Hall. Beyond it, another pillar matched the one they had already seen. It was backed by a Norman church with a crenelated tower, skirted by an attractive arched stone screen.

Before the arches people milled.

"Here's some fun at the butter market." Val gigged his mount into the midst of the crowd, calling back over his shoulder. "Come along."

"Wharton!" someone cried.

Heads turned. Smiles bloomed.

"Val!"

"It's our Valentine! Come home!"

"Happy birthday, Val!"

A good quarter of an hour, by the church tower's black-faced clock, was passed in vigorous handshaking and backslapping. Alexander and Oscar sat their horses, watching. Alexander thought again of the young woman. He could not stop thinking of her.

"Your name must go into the Valentine drawing and a shilling for the widows and orphans, Master Wharton." A gentleman who could be none other than the vicar waved a worn top hat, in which slips of paper fluttered.

Val nodded, grinning broadly. Whiskey sometimes made him playful in the mornings.

Oscar noticed. "A fine sight to see him smile again."

"Indeed. Up to mischief from the looks of it," Alexander said.

Two more shillings clinked into the hat. The vicar looked in their direction, calling out, "Two more Valentine heroes, ladies. And a good thing, too. We are short on gentlemen this year, with so many of the lads away with their regiments."

A feminine buzz acknowledged the truth of what he said, and more than one pair of curious eyes turned in their direction.

A lad stood ready to jot pencil to paper.

"Oscar Hervey," Val called out clearly. "A better fellow you'll never have the chance to meet, and . . ."

He paused, locking eyes with Alexander's, brows raised.

A shake of the head was all it took.

Val's smile widened. "And my good friend and comrade in arms, a gentleman whose shot always goes straight to the heart, none other than Cupid himself, ladies."

Gasps were followed by giggles and turned heads.

The vicar's brows rose. The boy's hand faltered.

Whispers and laughter swept the crowd.

"Valentine brings Cupid with him, does he?" someone shouted. Chuckles rumbled. The vicar beamed and nodded.

Oscar laughed and bowed, his arms and gaze sweeping in Alexander's direction, making it clear who Cupid was and wasn't.

"Well, ladies, a special Valentine indeed," the vicar chortled. "I think you'll agree. Shall we begin the draw?"

She walked into view at that moment, purple cloak catching in the wind, startling the liver brown pony, who went walleyed, rearing with a shrill whinny.

Alexander reacted instinctively. He turned the gray with no more than a squeeze of his thighs, the charger leaping with a clatter across the intervening cobbles.

Unnecessary heroics. She had the pony well in hand by the time he reached her. His hasty approach only set the smaller animal sidling and buck-hopping again.

Alexander reined in the gray and watched as Miss Touch-me-not soothed the beast with gentle words and firm hands.

"Again, I see you've no need of my assistance," he said, low-voiced, wondering if he was ever to know her name.

She nodded, the bonnet brim hiding her face, those eyes.

Behind him, the crowd fell still. Surprised, he turned

to meet a hushed strangeness—a closed quality in the faces of the women, a keen watchfulness in the men.

"Miss Foster!" the vicar cried out, voice uneven. "Shall we add your name to the hat?"

Nervousness flickered in the amethyst eyes. A strangely wordless creature, this Miss Foster. Fragile, he thought, easily broken. He found his gaze drawn to her again, and again he doffed his hat and turned the gray, returning to Oscar's side. Sliding looks followed him from those assembled, whispers passing furtively behind raised hands.

"Penny Foster," the vicar called as the lad added another slip of paper to the hat. "In she goes," he said. "Now stir it up well, Thomas."

The urchin plunged in his hand and made enthusiastic revolutions.

"And the first pair of Valentines is . . ." The vicar plucked from the hat, paused to unfold, to squint through his spectacles, paper fluttering. "Why, it is Penny Foster, and none other than . . . what does that say, lad?"

"Cupid!" the lad piped.

Over a sea of heads, their gazes met, as they had on the road, hers wary. Her cheeks flushed, and she raised her chin as if to block an oncoming blow.

"Cheap cherubim, to be had for a Penny," Val called sarcastically.

Laughter rippled.

"You've not stirred them enough, Vicar." A woman's complaint drew mumbled agreement from the crowd.

"What in the world has Val gotten us into?" Alexander asked.

Oscar chuckled. "Your line of work, Cupid, not mine."

"Shall I try again, then?" the vicar asked uncertainly.

Was it disappointment, or relief, that flickered

across Miss Foster's features? The vicar returned the slips to the hat and made a great show of tossing its contents most thoroughly, holding it out in the end to the lad, who dug his hand deep and emerged clutching two fresh bits of paper.

"Go on, Tom. Read them out."

Tom opened the slips and laughed.

"Don't be silly, lad," the vicar said. "Give us the names."

Tom laughed again.

"Oh, give them over, boy. We've a hatful yet to draw." The vicar snatched them from his grasp. "Miss Pe . . . Why, it's Penny again."

The crowd murmured disbelief, and more than once the phrase "bad ha'penny" might be heard.

The lad stopped his laughing long enough to say, "It's both of 'em again."

The vicar studied the second slip, and winked at Alexander. "It would seem this match is preordained, lad."

Murmurs and jests sounded.

Miss Foster looked his way, head cocked, then at the crowd, her mouth an unhappy line.

"Now what?" Alexander muttered.

Oscar plucked at his mustache and shrugged. "Don't ask me."

A young man called out, "And what would you be wanting for Valentine's Day?"

Alexander shrugged and called back, "Must I want something?"

Everyone laughed—except Miss Foster.

"Ask her, you dolt," Val whispered from behind him.

Ah! Now he understood. He cleared his throat. "What would you be wanting for Valentine's Day, Miss Foster?"

All talk in the square ceased that they might hear.

"What does every woman want on Valentine's Day?" she replied.

Her response stirred more ribald remarks and snide laughter.

The vicar raised his hands in a placating manner. "Now, now. Enough of that."

"How am I to answer that?" Alexander asked under his breath.

"She is to give three clues," Val explained dryly. "That was the first. Ask her again."

"And why do I ask?" Alexander wanted to know.

"Because you must in order to discover what she would have . . . as Valentine."

"I'm to give her a gift?"

"But of course." Val's response was unduly impatient.

"I have never played this game before, Val."

He blinked, then shrugged. "Oh! I am sorry you were not better prepared—or paired. She runs hot and cold, that one."

Oscar elbowed Alexander. "I've no idea of her temperature, but she is running."

She walked away briskly, the pony at her heels, every man present watching the sway of her purple cloak.

Alexander had no time to wonder what Val meant. "Wait, Miss Foster," he called. "You have yet to tell me what you want this Valentine's Day."

She stopped, and without turning, said, "But you are Cupid, sir, reputed to know every heart's desire."

"That's a clue?" Oscar muttered on the one side of him.

"It's supposed to be." Val's contempt was clear.

Alexander ignored them and tried again. "I wish to know *your* heart's desire, not every woman's."

His response drew an appreciative noise from the gathered women.

Miss Foster paused. She would not look at him.

"Simple, really," she said. "You have only to open your eyes."

She led Archer toward the blacksmith's, convinced he wished only to toy with her, convinced he was just like Val. He had not understood, any more than the others.

A breeze blew in off the Eden, smelling of wet stone and damp leaves—the smell of endings. Her life had been full of them. She drew her cloak closer. Hooves clopped against the cobbles behind her. The hairs at the base of her neck prickled. Lady Anne, protect me, she thought.

She knew it was him before he spoke.

His voice echoed in the empty street. "What would you have them see?"

She turned to find Cupid astride the big gray. Doomsgate had never seemed so narrow, and they two alone in it.

Persistent. She must give him that.

She took courage in his ignorance of her, and faced him as Lady Anne would have, determined he should see her as she wanted to be seen, not as everyone assumed she must be.

"What *does* every woman want on Valentine's Day?" he asked.

"What do you think?"

He slid from the saddle, and leading the gray, fell into step beside her. " 'Eyes,' you said."

His were green, dark and probing—the color of junipers. She found herself drawn despite her best intentions.

"Whose eyes must be opened, Miss Foster?" There was a hard edge to the question, to the set of his jaw.

"Does Cupid not know every woman's desire?" she asked rather than answer, breath hitching in her throat. He was smarter than she had bargained for.

He nodded, his expression serious, as if he took this

Valentine wish of hers very much to heart. "Every woman's desire? Why, what but love, Miss Foster, in a harsh and loveless world?"

"Loveless?" she asked, her features fresh, youthful, flowerlike—untouched by war.

He frowned, thinking of the men he had killed, of the unloving acts, of the grim aftermath of battle.

She backed away a step. Her mouth took on a troubled look. "You would declare yourself a failure, Sir Cupid?"

"In so many ways," he admitted, his gaze drawn to her mouth. He realized his frown was contagious as her lips took a downward turn. Pretty lips, full lips—he wondered if they had ever tasted love.

Her cheeks flushed. Lashes, thick and pale, cloaked the brightness of her eyes, as if she knew his thoughts.

"What does Cupid desire on Valentine's Day?" she asked.

He pursed his lips on a grin, and yet his eyes must have given away the thoughts that flooded his mind as he stroked the gray's nose, vastly inappropriate thoughts, all connected to her.

She flushed.

He asked, "Would you grant me a Valentine's wish?"

That valiant chin of hers rose.

His voice went throaty, seductive. "And me a stranger to you?"

The pony tossed its head and whickered.

She was not easily seduced. Wariness dominated her gaze as she replied, "Am I not a stranger to you? And yet, you would grant *my* wishes."

He loosed an amused and bitter sigh. "Yes, but I am Cupid."

"Is that so?" Brittle, her voice, chilly as the morning.

"Indeed."

"And Cupid has no Valentine wishes?"

"They aren't within your power," he said brusquely.

"Whose then?"

"God alone can give me what I desire, Miss Foster." He swung into the gray's saddle, then rode away without another word.

Chapter Three

She did not anticipate seeing him again that day; indeed, she resigned herself to the notion that once again the year would slip by without her Valentine wishes being given consideration, much less fulfillment, despite Val's return.

Jack, the blacksmith, a friend of her father's, who never failed in his kindness to her, followed her from the smithy, telling her the pony would be reshod within the hour should she care to return. "My name has been paired with Widow Brumley's," he complained. "I haven't the slightest notion what to get the old lady."

"Mrs. Brumley has a sweet tooth," she said. "Something from the confectioner's is bound to please."

His voice fell in asking, "And what sweet does yon sharpshooter bring you, then?"

"Sharpshooter?"

A man stood propped against the wall in the lane opposite, darkly handsome, something sharp and slightly dangerous in the way he waited, watching them. *Cupid!*

"Aye. That green cockade means the lad's a master marksman." Jack sounded impressed.

"Oh?"

He nudged her shoulder playfully. "Careful, lass, a canny one, that."

She wondered if he sensed it, too—the largeness of this marksman cupid, the agile turn of his mind, the undercurrent of danger. What would Lady Anne have thought of such a fellow?

"Miss Foster."

The muscles in this cupid's thighs, his calves, flexed provocatively as he pushed away from the wall.

"I must apologize."

With a wink, Jack returned to his anvil.

"Must you?" she asked, feeling abandoned and unexpectedly edgy in this stranger's company.

Thick lashes, dark as soot, long as a girl's, veiled his keen gaze. His voice fell. "I am not good company. Too long overseas, fighting. Too long in the company of men."

"Ah, but have you not heard? I am not considered good company either."

His head lifted. The breeze fingered his hair—not black as she had supposed on first seeing him, but deepest brown. He studied her a moment, in green-eyed surprise. Could it be Val had told him nothing?

A smile touched his lips, spreading slowly. "Is it true?" he asked.

She set off up the street, regretting the slip of her tongue. "I suppose I have been too long on the fells, in the company of none but my father, a taciturn man."

He fell into languid step beside her, the muscles of his legs and the shine of his boots fixing her attention.

His voice claimed her ears, low and gentle. "You asked earlier if you might fulfill my Valentine's wish, and I ungraciously refused you."

She slid a glance in his direction, wary, always wary.

"Perhaps I was wrong," he said.

She cocked her head. *What game was this?*

The deep green eyes studied her with every word, gauging her reaction. "I wish, while I am here, to walk the solitude of the lake—the fells—with someone familiar with them." He allowed the suggestion to hang between them.

She was no naive girl, as Lady Anne had once been, to be led astray by a rogue like the Earl of Dorset. "Val knows the area," she said firmly. "None better."

He laughed, a pleasant sound that rumbled deep within his chest, and yet she knew better than to trust a man's amusement. All too often they laughed at one rather than with one.

"Valentine is . . ." He frowned, choosing his words carefully. ". . . not a man given to silence."

"No," she agreed bitterly.

"Do you think . . ."

She knew what he hinted at, what he meant to propose.

"No," she stopped him.

All too serious the look in his eyes. "I wanted you—"

"I know what you wanted," she cut him off. "You want a young woman largely unknown to you to risk her reputation leading you onto the lonely fells."

He frowned. "No. I had heard—"

"That I've no longer a reputation to risk?" Bitter her words, bitter the sound of them.

He eyed her most keenly, his frown deepening. "No. That you've a man-eating dog to protect you."

Chapter Four

They settled into Wharton Manor as if it were meant solely for their recuperation, welcomed with quiet resignation by Val's parents, who gave them run of the place, passive planets dwarfed by the son. Lady Wharton kept herself largely confined to her sewing and embroidery room, while Lord Wharton closeted himself in his study, or rode the estate on the back of a stout-legged roan. They seemed, to Alexander, more like visiting guests in their own home than did their actual guests.

Val's parents appeared at the dinner table, and passed the young gentlemen in the corridors, but they were neither of them given to conversation, and when they did speak, it was always of the weather or some mention of the local doings. The war, just ended, was never mentioned.

The three comrades in arms took over the drawing room, where the decanters were kept filled on one of the sideboards, and into this domain the Whartons never intruded.

"You mean to go walking where?" Valentine asked in disbelief on their second evening together, the brandy decanter halted midair above his glass.

"The fells, the lakes," Alexander replied quietly, unsure what it was he read in Val's eyes. Strong emotion—just what emotion remained a mystery.

"With Penny Foster?" His friend laughed, sloshing

spirits. Was there anger in his eyes? "Did she ask it of you? Has the girl no shame?"

Shame? Alexander cocked his head, intrigued. What history did Val and Miss Foster share? There had been undeniable tension between the two on the road in their initial meeting.

And when Miss Foster had asked for what every young woman wants on Valentine's Day—was it something to do with Valentine Wharton?

"We must come along," Val suggested, setting down the decanter with a thump. "Else you shall have a devilish dull time of it." He smiled as he breathed in the brandy's perfume. His voice echoed a little in the hollow of the glass. "Miss Touch-me-not has meager conversation at best."

"So she warned me," Alexander agreed, swirling the contents of his own glass, determined to dissuade Val.

Val's brows rose. "Did she really?" He downed a gulp, smacked his lips appreciatively and shooed his mother's lapdog from a settee that he might seat himself. "You realize you are a lucky dog, to have been paired with her."

"How so?"

"Well, while there are half a dozen girls in the village I am sure you would find much prettier or more personable, you will not find another so ready to spread her legs for you."

Alexander blinked, stunned. He stood speechless, with the feeling his ears had just been boxed. Val's words were in every way offensive, and in some way incomprehensible.

"Town trollop, is she?" Oscar spoke from the depths of the chair in which he lounged.

Val assumed an irritatingly superior expression. "I cannot attest to the town, only to my own experience."

"Had her, have you?" Oscar downed the last mouthful of his brandy with relish.

Alexander sank into the nearest chair. *A trollop? Could it be true?* Nothing in his encounter with Miss Foster led him to believe Val's claim. Had she deceived him completely? Touch-me-not, Val called her.

"Threw herself at me, she did," Val contradicted the moniker. "Just before I bought my colors. I was only too happy to oblige."

Oscar chuckled appreciatively.

Val poured another brandy, then refilled Oscar's empty glass. Alexander waved the decanter away, waiting. There would be more. He knew Val well— the tales he enjoyed telling—the women he told them of. Handsome, charming Val was the top dog of their little trio when it came to winning women. He had left a trail of broken hearts in his wake. Or so he claimed. He had certainly taken his share of debauchery among the camp followers.

And this woman—this shy flower with the wary eyes—had he thrust himself upon her, obscene bumblebee?

Val strode the room, the brandy giving him the buzz of contentment. "Queer creature," he said. "Quiet as a child, then distant as a girl, the local mystery as a young woman. Kept close by her father, a local squire. Closemouthed sort. Has a bit of land, and the best flocks in the dale. I believe he owns an interest in the local mine. Shrewd. He has done quite well for himself, except when it comes to women, especially his wife."

"What of them?" Alexander asked.

Val savored his brandy, rolling the glass between his hands, swallowing with a contented sigh. "The lads noticed her eyeing me. Dared me to see where those looks might lead."

"What? You pinked the man's wife?" Oscar blurted, amazed.

Alexander, too, was caught up in the telling of this tale.

Val threw back his head to laugh. "Not the mother, the daughter. No, the mother . . ." He held his glass to the light, studying the liquid. "Ah. There was passion there, but not for me. Ran away with the gypsies when the girl was still in swaddling. They come every summer for our horse fair."

"And so the local lads decided the daughter ripe for the plucking?" Oscar suggested.

Alexander saw the way of it, the gossip that must have surrounded the girl, the speculation. "Did she take after the mother?" he asked.

Val laughed. "Moon-eyed for me, she was. Wanted loving. We had exchanged no more than a word or two before I kissed her."

Alexander rose and went to one of the windows. He needed air.

"She had no idea how to go about it," Val went on, no hesitation in sharing sordid detail. His lip curled. "A quick study, though."

Such nonchalance in the debauching of an innocent made Alexander sick to his stomach. The room seemed too close, too warm. He longed to step from this unpalatable reality into the cool dream of the misted landscape.

"You ruined her?" he asked quietly.

Val chuckled as he threw another log on the fire. "Wanted ruining, lad. Still wants it. You can see it in her eyes."

Alexander clamped his teeth on words that would have ended their friendship in an instant. He did not want to believe. And in his disbelief, all Val's boasted conquests were placed in question. Had the man lied all along?

"She does not seem the type."

"Type?" Val laughed. "They all want it. It is only

a question of when, and how much they would have you pay."

"How much did she want?" He hated himself for asking, but he had to know.

"Penny?" Val laughed, the sound of it brutal, callous. The same laughter that had followed every engagement of the enemy. Alexander had always assumed it a front for shattered nerves. Now he was not so certain.

"Her name says all." Val winked, then downed another gulp of brandy. "I had her cheap."

"She gave herself freely?" Alexander confirmed.

"A locket of my hair, a heart-shaped necklace to put it in, sweet words in the moonlight. As free as this."

Alexander closed his eyes on the misted view of the mountains. Val's details rang too specific to be disbelieved. "And did she love you?" he asked.

Val spread his arms, brandy sloshing. "All of them love me," he said. "Heaven knows why. She'll love you, too, given half a chance. You have only to ask. Go fell walking. See if she will not fall into your arms. I cannot think of any other reason to go traipsing about the countryside with the queerest, most awkward lass for miles."

Too strident the suggestion, Alexander mused. A bit of posturing. Was it the brandy talking?

"What say you, Oscar?" Val's words slurred. "Shall we take our Valentines fell walking? Make a party of it?"

"Count me out," Oscar muttered dryly. "Miss Fiona Gillpin does not look like she often enjoys exercise."

Val slapped his thigh with a boyish grin. "Ah, fat Fiona. I did forget with whom you are paired. She has grown considerable since last I saw her, and none of it vertically."

Oscar set aside his empty glass and joined Alexander at the window. "I have promised her two dances at the fete her father means to host this coming Friday. That is as much movement as I care for at present, unless it be with fishing pole in hand. I swear, lads, I have walked enough to last a lifetime. I shall never walk again where I can ride, and never attempt either if the weather is foul. If the skies are any indication, it promises to be foul."

Alexander found the rain-starred windows anything but foul. Here was a quiet, soft English rain, grown out of the mist. He had longed for just such rain while they were abroad.

"You will not want to walk the fells if it is wet," Val warned him. "Too easy a thing to slide about on shale. And if the sky is overcast, there is little view. Unless, of course, it is other hills and valleys you would explore."

Oscar laughed.

Coupled with Val's lewd innuendo, it irritated Alexander.

Oscar, watching, caught hint of his discontent and raised his brows in silent question.

Alexander forced a smile, wondering if it would not be better if hc just packed his bag and went home.

"Would you not rather come fishing?" Oscar asked.

"Or follow the Ullswater hounds in a foxhunt or two?" Valentine suggested, throwing companionable arms about their shoulders. "The quarry is cunning hereabouts, and as the hills are generally too steep for riding to hounds, a brisk walk is guaranteed."

Alexander recoiled inwardly. He could not tell Valentine he preferred a quiet, languid walk, and vast open spaces where neither gunfire, nor voices, nor the bark of dogs resounded. He could not tell his friends he felt completely estranged since their return, their common purpose no longer binding them, their common past receding. These two had watched his back— indeed, saved his life more than once—and he had returned the favor. They had shared muddy water, and the cleaning of bloody bayonets, and the daily fear that each moment might be their last. What did they share now?

The rain continued, postponing all outdoor entertainments, delaying the intrigue of his second encounter with Miss Foster, throwing Alexander into what Val considered the "excellent" company of any number of morning callers, for everyone must come to visit Master Wharton now that he was safe home from the fighting, and with him two intriguing strangers.

Most especially, three of Val's childhood chums made Wharton Manor ring with their voices. These boisterous young men were anxious to set out on a hunt when the weather cleared, anxious to recount the tale of a mad, wet ride that very afternoon when a prized mount's hock had been bruised in not quite clearing a stone wall. The owner, one Jeremy Leeds, hoped the horse would not have to be put down.

He seemed none too concerned, soon detailing the number of deer downed while Val was away, and birds, and rabbits. Anything that moved, it would seem. It was only when he had run out of tales of his own bloodletting that he evidenced an interest in hearing of the manhunt he had missed.

"Kill many Frenchies?" he wanted to know.

"Too many," Alexander longed to tell him, knowing the lad had no real idea what he asked. These ruddy-cheeked chubs did not want to hear regret, however. Bright-eyed, they waited, as anxious as hounds to the scent.

He held tongue, drifting to the half-open window that overlooked the dormant garden, his gaze drawn to the cool blue mist-shrouded hilltops, the chill breeze that stirred the draperies welcome against heated flesh. It would be dark soon, the gray afternoon sliding into grayer dusk, the sun never having pierced the clouds.

"It is Cupid you must ask about head counts." Val attempted to pull him back into the conversation. Alexander stepped closer to the swaying curtains. He had begun to regard the window as his safe haven—his escape. He braced his hands against a damply chill pane.

"A marksman, you see," Val bragged.

There were times like this when Alexander thought it was the braggable tally of his kill Val loved most in him.

He pushed the window higher with a squeal of swollen wood, closing his eyes to the sweet rush of cold air against his cheek, his hands. It swept damp, ghostly fingers down his sleeves and under the lapels of his coat.

"Bagged twice the number Oscar and I did combined. Was it only twice as many?" Val asked, his voice almost drowned out by the rattling flap of wind-kicked draperies.

Alexander leaned his forehead against the cool pane, studying the sill, the misted brick without. The ground was dark with the rain.

He had seen enough dark, wet ground for a lifetime, heard and seen enough of killing. He ducked his head to clear the window and stepped over the rain-dewed sill. He did not mind the wet, the cold.

How many young men had he stolen such a night from? How many clocks had he stopped? How sweet the privilege of rain-kissed cheeks, the smell of damp grass and sodden loam.

He did not stop when they called after him, did not even slow when Val warned him he would catch his death. They hung in the window a moment, deriding him for a wet fool. Why be soaked when one might sit warm by the fire?

He could not explain. They would not have understood. And so, he merely waved, saying, "I would stretch my legs a bit."

They closed the window behind him, shutting out the sound of bemused laughter, ribald jests, and cat-like yowling. They had their own ideas why he chose to wander. Val and Oscar had assumed the worst of him in Paris, then again in London, when he went walking for hours in the evenings, when he went looking for warmth and life and laughter, not in the arms of the ladybirds they themselves took comfort in, but in the lighted windows of the bourgeois—the framed mundane, where lamplight was all it took to hold the darkness at bay.

He walked for half an hour along the road, away from the manor, through the quiet village streets and beyond, reveling in the strength of his legs, in the heat within him exertion generated, in the unbroken stillness that fell along with the deepening gray of night. The rain stopped, and while the air was moist enough to bead the surface of his coat and waistcoat, and his boots splashed now and again through puddles pocking the road, he remained dry enough to avoid the shivers. Hands jammed deep in breeches pockets, shoulders hunched, he thought of other nights he had spent in the elements, grim nights that smelled of gunpowder and fear.

He closed his eyes for a moment, inhaling deeply the smell of wet pine, juniper, and rain-soaked earth. How beautiful the silvered gleam of moonlight breaking through thinning clouds. How wonderful the heated steam of his breath on rain-washed air.

He thought of Miss Foster as he had first seen her on this road. He had yet to fulfill her Valentine wish. That eyes should see.

No—that they should be opened. To what?

The cold bit at his nose, fingertips, and ears. He had never felt more alive. And yet he wondered, why had he survived among so many who had fallen?

The night gave him no answers.

He walked on.

He expected to share the darkness with no one, and yet, as he rounded a bend, hair prickled on the nape of his neck, and gooseflesh rose on his arms. He was not alone. Something moved ahead of him, a ghostly whiteness in the dark. On either side of him shale rattled. Childlike cries cut the darkness, the voices of the fallen. His pulse quickened, his heartbeat pounded in ears that strained to hear.

Ghostly white faces loomed.

He thought of the men he had killed.

Sheep crowded onto the road with clattering hooves and fearful bleats. They skittered away, frightened by his sudden laughter, disappearing on the uphill side, tails twitching.

The dog's low growl took him completely off guard. An animal cloaked by the night, he caught the quick gleam of its eyes, its teeth, heard unfriendly intent in the deepening rumble from its throat, and feared he would not walk away from their encounter unscathed.

A stick might save him—a stout stick, and none to be had, though there were rocks aplenty. A rock well placed might chase the beast away. He had only to scoop one up before the animal was upon him.

A whistle cut the darkness and a female voice murmured, "Artemis! Hush."

Her voice!

"Miss Foster?"

The dog stepped onto the road, a black-and-white collie, legs stiff, hackles raised, growling again, nose wrinkled, teeth displayed. The man-eater.

"Be still!" she ordered, though whether the direction was meant for him or the dog he could not say.

The dog sat, growls subsiding.

A darkness separated itself from the night, a bundled and hooded shape that seemed neither male nor female. "What business has Cupid here in the middle of the night?"

Her tone was forbidding. The dog muttered an

echoing discontent. Not the sound or manner of a woman given to passion and illicit midnight assignations.

"It is not so late as that, is it?" He pulled forth his watch.

The dog rose, teeth showing. Alexander fingered the gold fob. He might use it to throttle the animal if it lunged. "It has not yet gone ten."

The hood slid from her head. Moonlight made damply curled gossamer of her hair. "All of Westmoreland's abed at this hour," she said.

"But for you and me, wanderers of the night." He tucked away the watch, warmed by the image of that cloud of hair spread upon a pillow. *Damn Val.* He could not stop thinking of her in unmannerly terms.

The dog faced the way it had come, uttering a throaty sound.

Hobnailed heels clattered on sandstone. A man emerged from the darkness and paused to tip his hat to Miss Foster, to stare a moment in Alexander's direction before setting off with no more than a grunt.

"Not just you and I after all," she corrected him. "My shepherds have good reason to wander the night with fences downed by a careless jumper and sheep astray. Do you?"

Good reason? Was it not reason enough that he was alive? That he had two sound legs to carry him?

"I like to walk."

She stepped closer, her face silvered in the moonlight—wary. "So you say."

"You do not believe me?"

"I know next to nothing of you."

Was this wariness the manner of a fallen woman? Or did she simply not care for him? He did not want to believe either.

He squatted, holding his hand out that the dog might sniff. "Another archer, are you, pup?"

"She does not take to strangers," she warned him. "Especially men."

"Just as you do not?" he asked.

Her chin rose abruptly.

He looked back down at the dog. "An intelligent creature. It does not do to be too trusting of strangers—especially men."

Head cocked, lips pursed, Penny Foster patted her cloak, thigh level, drawing the dog to her side—drawing Alexander's attention to an area of her body he had best not think about. How easy would it be to spread the legs Val claimed to have conquered?

The dog leaned into the woolen folds of her cloak, within reach of her hand, bright eyes unwaveringly fixed, animosity unquenched.

She stroked the animal's head, murmuring low. Affection softened her voice and features, rousing desire within him for just such softness. It had been too long since he had been with a woman. When her gaze rose, amethyst eyes turned black by the night, her affections faded, swiftly replaced by the same wary watchfulness to be seen in the dog's eyes.

"Have you come to deliver my Valentine?" she asked, head cocked, a hint of vitriol in the question.

"Forgot to bring him," he said as a test, his tone in jest.

"Him?" she responded sharply.

"You do not care for Val?"

Her nostrils flared. "I have neither feelings, nor use, for him."

The crisp edge to her voice told him otherwise. She squatted to bury her fingers in the dog's thick ruff, to hug her neck in a manner most endearing.

"He told me he once held you in great regard."

She did not look up. "Did he? He has shown me no evidence of it." She gave the beast a kiss upon its forehead when it looked up. He envied the animal such affection.

"He said he might like to walk with us."

At that, she rose with alacrity. Artemis loosed a low, threatening noise and turned to glare at him.

"Would he?" Sarcasm laced her words.

"Shall I dissuade him?"

"That is entirely up to you." She motioned to the dog, sent her after the shepherd, without a word needed. Arms like crossed swords she clutched her cloak to bosom's swell, face lifted to the moon, profile girlish and soft, the sweet curve of her throat vulnerable. "Clear skies tomorrow."

His heart leapt at the prospect.

"Will you be in a mood for walking?" he asked.

She avoided answering the question, saying only, "The best time to view the local falls is after a rain."

"Which of the falls?" he asked.

She shrugged, drew the hood about her head, and turned in the direction her shepherd had disappeared, her voice growing fainter as she moved away. "Most are to be found in quiet places."

He wondered, as he watched her disappear into the darkness, what they might do, left alone together in a quiet place.

Chapter Five

Alexander woke before dawn the following day, anxious to see if Miss Foster's prediction of clearing skies might be true. He was ready for blue skies, for crisp, fair weather. It was a goodness that had too long been missing from his life.

From the breakfast room, where a maid brought him coffee and went away promising to have Cook put together a packet of food, he looked out on a garden just as cold and wet and misty as had met his eyes every other morning in Cumbria. And yet, in opening the window, he thought he smelled a change in the frosted air, and asked the butler, Yarrow, for directions to the most spectacular of the local waterfalls.

"Aira Force," the elderly gent said without hesitation. "It is a bit of a ride, but well worth it."

Alexander went to wake Oscar, who clutched his coverlet a little closer, asking, "Is it brown trout you are after?"

"No. A fine prospect. A waterfall."

His friend groaned and rolled over. "Leave the luxury of this warm bed for nothing more than a view? Count me out."

Alexander went next to his host's bedchamber.

"What? No warm armful to go with you?" Val croaked from the depths of his pillow.

Was Miss Foster the warm armful Val suggested?

"I go alone if you will not join me," Alexander said. He would not mind going alone.

Val waved him away. "Go, then. I've a splitting head."

"Too much brandy," Alexander suggested.

"Not enough," Val countered.

Content to enjoy solitude and the remote possibility of another encounter with the mysterious Miss Foster, Alexander mounted the gray and set off into the mists. He followed the Eden northwest as instructed, through frosted farm country where sheep bleated and apple trees and mossy oaks reached gnarled, dripping arms through the thinning mist.

The fells and hilltops, lost in the fog on either side of him, yet cast deep shadows in the dale. The promised sun was awhile coming, and when at last it bronzed the clouds above, he was well on his way, committed to the day's outing whether the skies cleared or not.

The sun warmed the shadows and burned away the mist, to the tune of the raven and the wren. Light burnished the shadowed flanks of the hillsides either side of him russet and fawn. Red deer skittered from the path as he approached, tails flashing. Red squirrels flitted through the treetops, chattering. Fog clung to the vales, misting last year's ferns with watery brilliance. Beneath the horse's hooves alder cones and acorns crackled.

The bony Pennines, to his right, cast harsh shadows on the fleshier, more feminine Cumbrian mountains to the left. The Eden chuckled wetly all the way to Temple Sowerby, a neat village, many of the houses recently built. There he crossed the river, noting the darting shadows of brown trout and salmon below. It was not quite fifteen miles to Penrith, a ride of an hour and a half. The sun warmed his back when he paused at the Two Lions for a drink and late breakfast. He was glad to rest the gray before they set off again into rising country.

It proved to be the morning he had hoped for, his solitude largely unbroken, no conversation to be made, only his thoughts, flowing like the river, a never-ending stream of the past. It was not until he reached the lake, Ullswater, that he thought again of sharing the day with another.

Miss Foster. She had drifted through his thoughts more than once as he rode, but in seeing the panorama of the lake spread before him, in setting out along its northwestern bank, he wished again and again that she were there, to tell him more of what he witnessed, to echo his awe, and most important, that he might discover more of her.

The past did not trouble him here. There was only room in his head for this moment, this beauty, this peace, and daydreams of the woman who brought him here, wherever she might be, whomever. The lake, long and narrow—hook-shaped—mirrored steep hillsides, cloaked in leafless, dripping hawthorn, alder, birch, and ash. Mosses and lichen faintly greened it. Gorse and heather had been browned by winter's touch. Frost silvered the venerable heights.

He and the gray took the path along the misted lakeshore at a languid pace, watching the waterfowl take flight at their approach: ducks, geese, moorhens, and coots. Herons stood one-legged in reedy shallows, cormorants lifted dark wings like cloaks to dry, while crested grebes postured like long-legged dandies, heads shaking, crests erect.

The peace he had longed for rode the wind here. It soaked its way up through the gray's legs, into his buttocks and thighs. It warmed his shoulders as the sun rose, dried the moisture that had beaded his overcoat, filled his ears with the gentle lap of water and the sigh of the wind. No shots to cut the silence, no boom of cannon fire. Here was England, and the

promise of growth, of life. Here his nostrils filled with
the wet odor of burgeoning earth. No death. No rot-
ting flesh. The knot inside his belly unwound as he
rode, the tightness in his shoulders relaxed. No need
to throw gun to shoulder here. No taste of powder on
his lips.

His thoughts drifted to the peace to be found in a
willing woman's arms. Miss Foster's? Would she open
herself to him, as this country did, unfolding fresh
beauties in every valley and dale, passion in her veins
like the rushing, white-watered becks feeding the great
placid heart of the lake?

One could always hope.

She saw the lone gray tethered in the wooded glen
where the path led to the waterfall and knew, heart
quickening, that he had followed her suggestion—and
that he came alone. She had imagined he would visit
the closest of the falls, Rutters. She had thought that
he would never ride so far for a bit of peaceful scenery. She would not admit that some part of her had
hoped he might come to Aira Force instead—hoped
and feared.

Now what was she to do? She drew the pony to a
halt, thought what Lady Anne might have done, and
sat staring at the gray.

Felicity tugged at the back of her cloak. "Is that Sir
Egremont's horse?"

Penny started, twisting to give the child a hand in
dismounting. "No, dear. Sir Egremont is but a character in a story." She unhooked her knee and slid from
the saddle.

"Once upon a time?" Felicity smiled up at her, pale
hair fluffing from beneath the edges of her bonnet,
cheeks like rosy pippins in the cold, reminding her of
herself at that age.

"Yes, dear. Once upon a time."

The child skipped to the signpost. "This way?" She pointed to the path.

"Yes, my dear. That way, but you will wait for me to hobble the pony, won't you, and stand well back from the beck?"

Felicity nodded, eyes bright with the excitement of their excursion, sturdy little legs carrying her away along the pathway despite her promise to wait. They had been horseback for more than two hours. Felicity had made the journey without complaint. A good child, not at all hesitant or fearful. Like her father. Penny wondered what Cupid would make of her.

Hands shaking, Penny laced the leather hobbles about the pony's hocks. She was not so brave as Felicity, never had been. *Well, perhaps once. A mistake, that.* Her courage had misled her. She looked forward with feelings of trepidation and misgiving to this encounter with Cupid. It even crossed her mind that it would be best if they did not meet. She could ride home again, and visit the falls another day.

Felicity decided the matter for her. By the time the hobbles were tied, she was nowhere to be seen. Penny's heart lurched. She thought suddenly of her mother. Her feet stumbled into motion.

The sloping path was familiar, slippery where wet, awkward as it wound through tree roots and under low branches. The force revealed itself a little at a time, through the trees, a boil of white accompanied by the growing noise of moving water—rushing, falling, eternal. *Dangerous. Where was Felicity?*

She raced through the grove, sunlight blinded her in flashes. There, just ahead, standing too close to the beck of course, a basket at her feet, a twig in hand, poking at a jug that had been left to cool in an eddy in the swift-flowing water.

"Felicity!" she called. "I asked you to wait, to stay well back from the water."

The child turned with guilty expression, as if startled by her own waywardness.

"What's this?" she asked.

"Someone's supper. Come away now."

She obeyed, a trifle dejectedly. "I'm hungry," she said.

"Come then. We shall have a look at the force first, and then we shall ride to the nearest inn for a bite to eat. Unless you wish to eat first? Come back later?"

She half hoped Felicity would nod. Instead, with an impish smile, the child grabbed her hand and dragged her toward the noise of the falls.

The sound wrapped itself around them, loud enough that he did not hear them approach, though Felicity cried out "Pretty!" when they came within sight of the force.

Penny had known he would be there, but was not at all prepared for the sight of him. He stood, as if bewitched, beneath a rainbow. It arced through the mist kicked up by a torrent of water that boiled and slid down the hillside, seventy feet or more, water gone milk white it flowed so fast. He stood with his back to them, at the second of two vantage points that overlooked the spectacle, head thrown back, expression rapt. A magical sight—the rainbow, the white water, his awe.

Felicity's little legs stopped moving. Grip tightening, she stared, as struck by the image as Penny.

"Have no fear." Penny drew her onward. "It is only Cupid. He will not bite."

She thought he would turn—notice them. He did not, simply stood, entranced, fixed as a statue, in his very stillness entrancing.

Cupping hands to mouth, she shouted, "Halloo!"

The sound of rushing water swallowed her cry. He did not respond.

"Did Emma fall from there?" Felicity pointed to the spot where he stood.

"Perhaps," she said, considering the matter with a sigh, thoughts of her mother tumbling like the water.

Felicity stared unwaveringly at Valentine's Cupid. "Will your friend fall?"

Again Penny thought of her mother. She frowned. "I do not think so, dearest. Are you still hungry? Shall we go?"

"Does he know?" she persisted.

"Know what?"

"About Emma?"

"I . . . I do not know."

"Will you tell him?"

Such a solemn face the child had when she was worried.

"A grown man knows to be careful on wet rocks, dearest."

She did not look convinced, her dear little face was tender with concern.

Penny sighed. No getting around it. She would have to go and speak to him. Felicity would fret all of the way home if she did not. And if he did fall—well, she, like her father, would never be able to forgive herself.

"You will wait here? And I do mean right here." Penny knelt, her tone impressing upon the child the seriousness of her instruction. "I will go and tell him. But you must not budge an inch. The path is very slippery ahead, and I would not have you fall while I go and tell my friend that he must not. Right?"

Felicity, wide-eyed, nodded, eyes locked on the stranger, the troubled look easing from her brow.

Penny went to him, careful of her footing, glancing back over her shoulder now and again to assure herself Felicity stayed put. The child stood like a statue, watching. It was wet this close to the water's spray, a trifle dizzying, the beck rushing, rushing, rushing, in a steep, tumbling race with itself through a narrow chasm of moss green stone and water-bared tree roots. Something in the sound matched that of breath and pulse as she went to him, anxious to return to the child, her gaze and attention divided. The water drew her, the sight of him, too, the damp sheen of his hair wafting in the breeze stirred by plunging water.

He turned at last, forehead, cheeks, and lips misted, a gleam in his eyes. He moved to meet her as she navigated the last of the pathway, his hand clutching her elbow as her shoe skidded on mossy stone.

"You came!" She saw his lips move, all sound drowned by the voice of the force.

He stepped nearer to hear her response, his hand still at her elbow, head bent close, the look in his eyes soft and bright and slippery all at the same time, like the moss beneath their feet. "You came."

She heard him that time, his breath warm on her cheek.

It had been a long time since a gentleman had looked at her as Cupid did now. She stared a moment, marveling, lost in his eyes.

"Yes, I had to . . . I had to . . ." She wet her lips, mouth gone cottony.

He did not allow her to finish. The gleam in his eyes brightened. The hand at her elbow slid to her waist. He caught her off guard, leaning forward suddenly, his kiss strong—urgent—a match for the force's rushing fervor.

It took her breath away. For the length of a sigh, she succumbed to the damp need of his mouth, the answering need of her own.

Good sense returned, and fear. She thought of Val, of Felicity—of Eve.

Pushing roughly at the firm warmth of his chest, she struck his cheek as hard as she might in kid gloves. The bones of her hand ached with the flat-handed strength of it, even as she whirled, saying, "Is this why they call you Cupid?"

Too fast, her move on slippery rock.

"No. Another reason." The words seemed distant, blurred.

Her hands windmilled, but found no ready purchase. She felt herself falling. Like Emma, like Mama. Oh, God, not like Mama, not in front of the child!

Below her, Felicity screamed.

He grabbed the tail of her coat in the last instant, fabric stretching taut, seams straining, threads popping under her arms as her heart leapt into her mouth and the plunge of water beckoned, dizzyingly.

The child gazed up through bare branches, her mouth a rounded O.

With a firm yank Cupid altered her view, pulling her back against his chest with a shoulder blade–jarring thump.

"Not so fast," he said. "There is a better way down."

"Dear God." The words sighed from her lips. "She ought not to have seen that."

"The kissing, or the falling?"

She laughed, a nervous release. "Either."

His cheek bore the imprint of her hand, faintly pink. She scowled at it. "I do apologize for striking you, and thank you—"

"For the kiss?" His eyes twinkled.

"For saving my life."

"I would rather you thanked me for the former." His breath on her ear was almost as provocative as his lips had been. "I, too, must apologize. I thought you came alone."

Shaken, she stepped from his arms, with care for her footing this time, her gaze fixed on Felicity, to whom she waved, forcing herself to smile. "That would be as foolish as falling headfirst into the force," she shouted over her shoulder.

"Dangerous, am I?" he shouted back.

She turned to look him in the eyes. Dizzying, they

were, dangerous. She feared falling into the deep green pools as much as she had into Aira Force.

He stepped closer.

"I came to warn you," she said, holding her ground, wanting him to hear, "not to fall."

"Too late." He leaned closer to say it in her ear. Laughter played in his voice and in his eyes as she stepped back. "I fear I have already fallen."

The suggestion in his voice took her breath away. Like his kiss. Her gaze was drawn to his mouth. Then she looked away. "Do you read Wordsworth?" she called out to him as she set off again.

" 'Strange fits of passion have I known:' " he quoted, hard upon her heels, " 'and I will dare to tell . . .' "

She stopped. He almost bowled her over, no choice but to catch her in his arms once more with that same brightness of eye that had led to a kiss.

" 'But in my lover's ear alone . . .' " he whispered in her ear, the words like the kiss, firing a dangerous warmth.

" 'The Somnambulist'?" she asked abruptly, pushing from his arms, stepping away.

He shook his head. "Don't know that one."

"He tells of a young woman named Emma who fell in love here."

"Oh?" His voice still held laughter, and the suggestion of something seductive.

"With a gentleman named Sir Egremont."

"How romantic."

She shook her head and dared to look him in the eyes again. "A tragedy really. He went away to war before they were wed."

His mouth tightened at mention of war. The light in his eyes diminished. "Did he return?" he asked, jaw tight.

"He did," she answered, "to find that in his absence Emma's mind had come unhinged with worry."

He frowned.

"She had begun to walk in her sleep, and one of the places she walked was here, where they had spent happy moments."

His attention was complete, and yet his brow furrowed a little as if he did not comprehend the connection she implied. She regretted more than ever the imprint of her hand upon his cheek.

"Did she recover?" he asked.

Penny sighed. "Hearing of her altered state, he came looking for her the evening of his return. She was here, above the falls. He called her name, startling her."

"She fell?" he guessed.

She nodded.

His jaw twitched.

"Broke her neck, and his heart," she said. "He became a hermit, gave up all his worldly possessions, and lived out the rest of his days in a cave."

"A good thing I caught you," he said, and when she looked at him quizzically, he went on, the seductive twinkle returning to his eyes. "I do not care for caves."

Chapter Six

"And *I* do not care to be kissed by strangers." She turned her back to him.

"Really?" He cupped her elbow as she stepped over a tree root, leaning close to whisper, "I got the impression otherwise."

She turned, eyes flashing, the ribbon of rushing water a perfect backdrop for the fire in her gaze. The air smelled slightly musky, of wet stone and molding leaves. His mouth tasted of her. He wanted more. He wanted in that instant for her to be the wanton Val claimed, for if she were, he might have her, and soon.

"You are mistaken," she snapped.

She had not recoiled from his embrace. Her lips had gone deliciously soft beneath him.

"I am, myself, excessively fond of kisses," he admitted, refusing to catch the contagion of her anger, curious to see her response.

The words widened her eyes, and then, lashes sweeping down to hide her surprise, she walked away.

He stood a moment, admiring the slope of her shoulders, the graceful bend of her waist, the sway of her hips. A trim ankle she exposed in lifting her skirts from the wet.

She called back over her shoulder, "Is this a cupid's compliment? Do you kiss anything female that comes within arm's reach?"

"Not at all," he said. "I am very particular."

"What is your real name?" she demanded without

stopping. "I cannot continue to call you Cupid, though Cupid you may consider yourself."

"Alexander," he said. "Alexander Shelbourne. Same as my father before me."

He could not be sure she heard him. On she went, dodging branches, setting a pace that gave him the feeling he chased her, and chase her he would, to set things right between them, to express in some way his gratitude that she had allowed him to save a life instead of taking it. That she had renewed within him a lust for living.

The fair-haired child jumped up and down with ill-contained excitement as they approached, worry covering features that reminded him of Miss Foster's— same breadth of forehead, same snip of a nose. "I stayed," she said breathlessly, fingers worrying the chain about her neck. "Right here. Even when you slipped, just like Emma. I thought you would fall."

"Indeed, so did I, my dear. This is Mr. Shelbourne, who saved me." She turned to him at last, her hands on the girl's shoulders. "Mr. Shelbourne, this is Felicity."

"Felicity Foster." She curtsied with all the grace of a well-schooled five-year-old.

He bowed, eyes fixed on the flash of gold at her neck, a locket, heart-shaped.

Foster? What relation, he wondered. Val made no mention of a child, only of just such a locket, given to Penny Foster on a night of shared passion.

"Pleased to meet you," he said. "You may call me Shel, as my sisters do, or Cupid, as does the whole of my regiment."

The younger Miss Foster looked uncertainly at the elder.

"You may do as you wish, my dear," she said.

"Is it true?" the girl lifted her face to him. "You must give Penny a Valentine?"

Penny, not Mama. Was the child not hers?

"Felicity." Mild reproof in the elder Miss Foster's tone, a motherly sound.

Alexander knelt to study the girl, seeking definitive proof of her parentage in her pretty little face. "Can you tell me what Valentine Penny wants?" he asked.

"No, she cannot," Miss Foster said decisively.

"A pity." He rose. "I do not like to remain indebted. People might get the mistaken impression I've no intention of honoring my commitments."

Miss Foster bit her luscious lower lip. He did not like to see it thus abused.

"The small matter of this Valentine does not matter, Mr. Shelbourne," she murmured.

"I beg to differ." Still he studied the child, considering the curl of ashen hair, like Val's. Not like Miss Foster's. "Small things can make all of the difference in the world. If they are misunderstood, misrepresented, or confused, mistaken assumptions follow. I have known lives to be lost for less."

She regarded him a moment with the uniquely amethyst-colored eyes.

The child's were blue.

"In some instances," she said, "perhaps you are right. In this case, you make too much of it, sir."

"Do I? I am not convinced. You see, in the small matter of my name, just such a misunderstanding might arise. You call me Mr. Shelbourne, rather than the more familiar Shel, or Cupid. One might think you mean to distance me."

"One might," she agreed.

"I'm hungry," the little girl complained.

"Come, then. We shall go." She meant to abandon him. She took Felicity's hand and set off briskly along the path.

"I've food enough for the three of us," he said, hoping to stop her, wanting to spend more time in her company.

The child paused and looked back, only to be

yanked into motion again by Miss Foster's steady progress.

"But, I'm thirsty—"

"We thank you, Mr. Shelbourne," Miss Foster said stiffly. "But I fear we must decline your kind offer. We mean to visit the nearest inn."

"That is miles away," he protested.

"Miles?" A whine in earnest. The child's discontent became his ally. He did not hesitate to use it.

"A half hour, at best, before you find such a place."

"Is it so far?" The child sounded pitiably forlorn.

"A half hour is nothing," Miss Foster said to bolster the girl's flagging patience.

"And another half hour before the food is served." He played devil's advocate.

Her pace did not slow. She shook her head. "I do not think—"

"It really requires no thought." He had no intention of allowing her to leave. "You could relax beside the lake and feed the child."

"I'm thir-rr-sty," the little girl said.

"We shall cup some water from the beck."

"I've milk," he suggested.

"Milk?" Miss Foster stopped so fast he almost ran into her. She turned in her tracks, gazing at him with frowning skepticism, much like the moment in which he had bent to kiss her. "You have milk?"

"In the jug in the beck?" the child asked.

"Yes."

Miss Foster's brows rose.

"You do not strike me as a milk drinker, sir."

"I thought, if I should have the good fortune to encounter you here, that you might like it in your tea."

Silence as she absorbed this.

"Darjeeling or China black? I've a camp kettle to boil water."

She frowned, uncertainty clouding her brow, defenses breached.

"If nothing else, let the child have a drink before you go," he suggested.

She sighed, ready to succumb. He delivered the *coup de grace*. "I will press you no more. It matters too much to me that we should remain friends."

Her frown became more pronounced. "Were we ever?" she asked frankly.

"Were we not?" He turned the question back on her.

She pursed her lips. "I know too little of you to regard you as friend, Mr. Shelbourne. I have only just learned your name."

"Oh? I knew from the moment we met we were to be friends." His lips, gone dry now, remembered the moist, willing potential of her mouth. They had already stepped beyond the limitations of mere friendship. She knew it as well as he, and he was not going to let her run away from that without a struggle. "We've no chance of any kind of relationship if you cannot forgive me," he pointed out.

She looked at the child. *Val's child?*

The child looked back, her desire for food and drink hovering in a soulful gaze.

"Forgiveness is a quality worth nurturing," Penny said. "You must remember that, Felicity."

He wanted to kiss her again—for capitulating, for any reason whatsoever, and no reason at all.

The girl's face brightened. "Shall I run and fetch the jug?"

"Ask Mr. Shelbourne."

He nodded.

"Go then."

She skipped ahead, Miss Foster watching, love in her eyes.

"A pretty child," he said. "She looks like you."

"Do you think so?" The brilliance of her gaze dimmed. "I see so much of her father in her."

"Do I know him?" he asked carefully.

She studied him a moment before responding with an enigmatic smile. "I do not think you do."

Not Val then. Not the love child he had feared she must be. "He leaves her care to you?" He had to know more, and yet he would step lightly over heavy ground.

"Entirely."

Beyond that, she was not forthcoming.

"About your kisses, Mr. Shelbourne." She effectively diverted his attention.

His brows rose involuntarily. "My kisses, Miss Foster?"

She blushed, then looked away. "I would not have you think I encourage them."

He let the words hang between them a moment, tension building. He watched the pulse beat faster in the vein in her neck. "Not at all," he said at last. "I understand they discomfited you."

"Yes." She looked up.

"Such was never my intention."

"No. I'm sure you were led to believe I would welcome them."

"I was not led at all," he countered. "I simply charged in where I was not yet wanted. Can you forgive me?"

Her eyes, those remarkable amethyst eyes, fixed on him in a manner most provocative, though he was certain that was not at all her intention.

"This time," she said.

He found himself distracted by her mouth—the mouth that he must kiss again, and soon.

"I trust that I shall never need to forgive you again," she said.

He nodded, bowed, and vowed to himself that the next time he kissed her, forgiveness would prove unnecessary.

Chapter Seven

They chose a patch of sunshine, sheltered from wind, with a view of the lake. The force made a distant hushing noise, the lapping of the lake overriding it. He built a fire, boiled water, made tea, and poured milk for the child into a telescoping cup. With the smell of wood burning in the open air, military campfires came to mind. He frowned, no desire to remember.

"Are you all right?" she asked.

He shook away the past, poured her a mug of tea, and set the camp kettle in the coals.

"Never better." He forced the cheer with which he chose to supplant all melancholy. "I must thank you for agreeing to stay, for suggesting this place. It is . . ." His voice faded.

"Beautiful?" Her gaze fixed on the lake.

He studied with fascination the golden glitter of sunlit hair against the water's silvered shimmer.

"Sublime."

She turned, her eyes changeable as the water, questions there.

"I would not have enjoyed it half so much alone," he said.

"What did you bring to eat?" the child interrupted.

Penny quickly corrected Felicity for her forwardness.

Val's cook had provided mutton sandwiches, apple tarts, a crock of mustard, another of chutney. Simple fare, but tasty. The child ate heartily, then looked skyward, asking him to identify all of the birds she could spy. She had a keen eye. It was an hour before she lay her head in Miss Foster's lap and snuggled close for a nap, clutching the locket, the bothersome heart-shaped locket.

He poured fresh cups, then sat back to enjoy the aromatic brew that warmed him as much as the sight of Penny Foster stroking the child's hair away from her brow, the little girl's face gone slack with sleep—both of them tender, vulnerable, beautiful.

Miss Foster looked up, her face shuttering away that tenderness, her eyes wary, always wary, when she looked at him, like a hunted animal. He had seen that same fear in men's eyes, in hand-to-hand combat. He did not like to think he provoked it in her, now.

"Tell me about the lake," he suggested. "These peaks. Have they names?"

"Place Fell." She twisted to point, careful not to wake the child. "Hellvelyn. Stybarrow Dodd, and Great Dodd backed by Fairfield and Great Seat." The russet flanks were grayed by distance. Her hand swept northward, over her shoulder. "Loadpot Hill."

He smiled. "Odd name."

She nodded, smiling back at him, his heart touched by the sight of those lips upturned. She looked across the lake. "Then there is Little Mell Fell."

"Mustn't forget that," he murmured.

She blushed, then turned serious, telling him of lead mines near Glenredding, and the damming of Goldrill Beck, and the forests of Glencoyne, the names like music on her tongue, her love of the place undisguised.

"There is a tower, there." Again she pointed, and he found himself far more fascinated by the tilt of her wrist, and the curve of her back, and the curls of golden hair that blew in the wind than in the Duke of Norfolk, who had built a hunting lodge.

"And over there . . ."

She twisted. He breathed deep as her movement revealed the swell of breast and hip, a bit of cleavage.

"A pre-Roman ruin," she said. "Dunmallard Hill is difficult to see for the trees, but Romans, Saxons, Celts, Vikings, Norsemen, and Scots have fought to hold it."

He closed his eyes, imagining the clash of swords, the echo of gunfire from the slopes.

"One cannot escape it," he muttered.

"What?" she asked mildly.

"Man's violence." His bitterness was real, each word clipped. "His need to conquer, possess, and kill."

With a stricken look, she covered the sleeping child's ears. "Yes," she said. "But that is the past."

He rose, startling a flock of ducks, their muted honking striking fear in the grebes and cormorants, all of them taking wing, a flock of angels rising, their combined wing beats enough to wake the dead.

The child opened her eyes with a moan.

He regretted his sudden move, regretted unsettling the peace of the lake, regretted the violence of his words.

So much to regret. So very much to regret.

Chapter Eight

He rode in silence for the first half hour of their return journey, a weight of thoughts hanging about his head like a dark cloud.

The gray horse set the pace for their steady trot, long tail swishing. The pony kept up well enough.

His leg, slightly higher than her own, on the taller animal, drew Penny's eye. Well-muscled and rock hard, clad in breeches that clung, it was a limb worthy of study, the leg of a man who had spent hours in the saddle.

She did not try to fill the silence, but simply watched the flex and bulge of muscle, wondering if he tired of her company, of their company.

Felicity, the little magpie, chattered nonstop, spewing questions unending about the trees, the clouds, and the squirrels that skipped across the road ahead of them in quick, red flashes. She responded patiently, quietly, wondering if their conversation disturbed him.

He roused at last as they crossed the bridge at Temple Sowerby, when she asked, "Do you mean to fish while you are here, Mr. Shelbourne?"

He broke his speechless reverie with a puzzled grimace. "Fish, Miss Foster? It is Oscar who is mad for fishing. Why?" He eyed her up and down, as if imagining her in gumboots, rod and creel in hand. "Do you enjoy angling?"

"For safe topics, yes."

His gaze sharpened. He shifted in the saddle and

looked past her, toward Cross Fell. "I am poor company," he apologized.

She sighed. "Lost in thought. I often do the same. What were you thinking?"

His hands, for miles so still, now fingered the reins uneasily. "I fear I dwell too much on the past."

"The war?"

He nodded. His gaze flickered in Felicity's direction. "Things best forgotten."

She considered for a fleeting moment what it must have been like. His concern for the child touched her. "I appreciate your sensibilities, sir, but surely such events must never be forgotten."

His brows rose.

She stroked Archer's mane, the dark hair, coarse and long, felt wonderful between her fingers. She wondered what Mr. Shelbourne's hair felt like. She wondered if she had offended him. "I have never been to war, but I find, in my own trivial conflicts, I come to better understand myself and human nature, good and bad."

He studied her a moment, his deep green eyes unreadable—she could not tell if he thought more or less of her for her remark, only that it would seem to have startled him.

"I am not one for chitchat, Mr. Shelbourne." She wondered if he expected some kind of apology for her outspokenness. "I find it a waste of breath, thought, and energies."

"Indeed?" His eyes narrowed.

Had she said too much? Spoken too freely? It was what she considered both a strength and a failing, voicing her opinion, especially when it ran contrary to common beliefs or practice. It had earned her something of a reputation. She was in addition to her questionable status with regard to Felicity, and her mother, considered an oddity for her own sake. Eccentric. Had Lady Anne been considered thus?

"Whose eyes would you have me open, Miss Foster?" he asked abruptly. "And to what end?"

She frowned. He raised the one topic in which she did not care to delve And yet, she had asked for this. She could not now refuse him.

"The world's eyes, sir," she said simply, "to who and what I am."

"And what is that?"

She bit her lower lip. "An unfit topic," she said elusively.

He glanced beyond her, to Felicity, clinging quietly, listening. The child soaked up everything.

"You set me a difficult task." He shifted in the saddle, thigh muscles flexing, driving all thought and sense from her for a moment.

"Yes." She laughed. "Perhaps impossible."

"Who are you?" he asked.

She lifted her gaze from the strength of his thigh to find him regarding her with intense curiosity, and a gleam of mischief in his eyes.

"You know me, sir."

"Not really. I know your name, and that you like Darjeeling tea better than China black, and fells better than dales, but above and beyond that . . ." His eyes scanned the horizon, a distance yawning between them, a sudden chill. She had seen that look before in his eyes, at the campfire.

He blinked and shifted his gaze, the look fading. "Do we any of us really know one another?"

"Given time, the truth, and desire," she said without thinking how the last word might be misinterpreted.

He smiled, mischief returned, nothing distant in the look he bent on her in saying, "We have the time. I am beset by desire—as to truth—that is up to you and me. I thought we might address what and who you really are. By what deeds you would be known."

Who was she? Simple as that, and yet, not so simple.

She thought of Lady Anne, of the influence of two dead women.

"What makes a person?" she asked. "There is so much ground to cover."

"Past, present, and future," he agreed.

"And more."

Felicity's little hands were hot on her back. So much more, she thought.

"Connections," he added. "Family and friends."

Yes, family, she thought, though she could not tell him how. Not yet. She did not know if she could trust him yet with so much.

"Dreams and desires." Her voice sounded unintentionally wistful.

He cocked his head, dark green eyes considering her, the corners of his mouth downturned. "Will you share yours with me, Miss Foster?"

Felicity spared her from answering by inserting herself into their conversation. "I like waterfalls," she announced.

He evidence neither irritation nor impatience, saying in the gentlest of voices, "They make a lovely noise, don't they? Like the hush of the wind through the trees, or the tide on a sunny day."

"Is it?" Felicity wondered. "I have never seen the sea."

"Nor I," Penny echoed.

"What?" He stared at them, amazed. "Tucked away in the fells all of your life? I must take you both to the seaside someday."

"May we?" Felicity asked, eyes bright.

Penny laughed. "We must first introduce Mr. Shelbourne to the fells."

"Do his friends mean to come?"

Penny waited his answer.

He shook his head, leaning from the saddle, his knee accidentally bumping hers, as he chucked the child under the chin. "They prefer chasing after fishes and foxes."

In his mischievous smile, in his easy, affectionate exchanges with the child, Penny found herself liking Alexander Shelbourne more than she ever might have expected. Was this how it had been for Lady Anne and the Earl of Pembroke?

"How did you and Val become friends?" she asked.

His head jerked up with unexpected speed. His smile wavered. "He saved my life," he said. "I'll tell you about it someday. And you?"

"And me, what?"

"Fell for him, did you?" He watched her keenly.

How did one respond to such a question?

"Most women do," he said.

Penny shrugged. "He led me . . ."

His brows rose. The word "astray" seemed to hang between them, and that was not at all the impression she wished to give.

She frowned. "He led me to believe he cared for me. I was naive, trusting. But that was years ago. I am sure Val has changed as much as I have."

He nodded. "You've had a falling out?"

"We have," she allowed.

She tried to reconcile what she knew of Val with the heroism Alexander mentioned so nonchalantly. She must, she thought, let go of the past.

"I am glad to hear he was in a way to save your life, just as you were in a way to save mine today." *Oh, Lady Anne*, she thought. *There is hope for us all if Valentine Wharton is a reformed man.*

Chapter Nine

Alexander did not go fell walking the following day. Clouds sat heavily upon the dale, and did not lift. He and Val took Oscar fishing, and as they cast their lines into the rain-dotted Eden, he asked Val, "How long ago did you leave the dale?"

"All of six years," Val said readily enough.

"And is it changed?" Oscar wondered.

"Not a bit," Val said. "Other than that we are all older. How went your jaunt yesterday, Cupid? Was the force in full force?"

"Splendid," Alexander said. I chanced upon a familiar face."

"Did you? Who?"

He had both their attention.

"My Valentine," he said, picturing her the moment he had kissed her, savoring the memory.

"Touch-me-not? Chasing after you, is she?"

Was it jealousy colored Val's voice as he jerked his line from the water and cast it impatiently to a new spot? Alexander wondered.

"She was there with a child," he said, casting truth at Val, hoping he might catch more of it, if he was patient.

"Child? What child?"

"I cannot claim to be entirely clear on that point. She is a Foster, in the care of your Miss Foster."

"Not *my* Miss Foster at all anymore, my friend," Val protested. "*Your* Miss Foster it would seem. As to the child . . ." His lips pursed, his voice dripped with even more sarcasm than usual. "A by-blow, most likely. Does she favor Touch-me-not?"

"She is fair, with blue eyes."

Val shook the fair hair from his own blue eyes. "And how old did she appear to be?"

Alexander shrugged, though he was not at all casual in studying Val's hands gripping the pole, his knuckles gone white. "Difficult to tell. I do not consider myself a good judge when it comes to children, but she does not look to be more than five or so."

If Val had any response in mind, it was cut short by the salmon that struck hard on the end of his line, but Alexander wondered many times afterward if it was the bite of the fish, or the news he had just received, knocked Valentine Wharton unsteadier in that instant.

Penny saw him while crossing the bridge over the River Eden, he and his two friends walking toward her, fishing creels slung across their shoulders, rods piercing the ground-hugging clouds. Fine-figured young men, all three of them, and yet at sight of them her attention fixed exclusively on Alexander Shelbourne, on the dark gleam of his hair, the strength of shoulder and thigh, the narrowness of waist and hip. She awaited his reaction to the sight of her with pent-up breath.

He was speaking to Oscar Hervey, head bent, shoulders shaken by laughter as Oscar's hands gestured. Oscar spotted her first and stopped talking. The dark head rose, hollow cheeked. The depths of his gaze turned first to Oscar, and then, sensing her approach, toward her. And suddenly, she could breathe again, deep, happy breaths, for his first reaction was to smile, a broad, face-brightening smile, as if it were the most natural thing in the world—as if he could not have stopped himself from smiling had he tried.

Cupid, her Cupid, raised his pole in salute, and quickened his pace.

Valentine Wharton did not.

Oscar simply eyed her with keen interest, his gaze straying now and again to regard his companions.

"If it isn't the Misses Foster," Shelbourne called out jovially.

"Cupid!" Felicity squealed, and slipping Penny's hold, ran toward him. "We have been to market," she said.

"Have you?" He knelt to speak to her on her own level. "We have been fishing."

"Catch anything?" she asked, leaning into his bent knee.

"Look and see," he suggested, his gaze rising to meet Penny's as Felicity lifted the creel lid with a gasp.

"Trout!" she cried. "And salmon. Three big ones."

"Luck, Mr. Shelbourne?" Penny asked, self-conscious under the eyes of so many. As glad as she was to see him, she meant to keep the encounter short—safer that way—smarter—and easier on her nerves.

"Indeed," he agreed, gazing at her over Felicity's fair head with a twinkle in his eyes meant just for her. Did their encounter figure into that luck somehow?

Then Val was upon them, nothing lucky in the chill gaze he fixed on either of them. "So you've a child, have you, Penny, since last we met?"

Lady Anne, Lady Anne, she thought. She must not let him rattle her with his bitter suggestiveness, not with his friends, not with Cupid watching so intently. Not with Felicity staring up at them. "A child in my care, yes, Val. A lot has happened since you went away."

The man that had once won her with a lad's wink regarded her as coldly as if they were complete strangers.

"Whose is she?" he asked bluntly.

She could have slapped him. Felicity's attention was

by now firmly fixed on the two of them, her keen little ears taking in every word, her body tense with listening.

"She is mine, now. Aren't you Felicity, my love?"

She took the child's hand, her gaze meeting briefly that of Mr. Shelbourne as he rose, lacing his creel lid shut.

"Little pitchers have big ears, Val." He curtailed Val's response in asking, "Can these questions keep? Fish are spoiling."

Penny was thus spared further questions, further contact of any kind with Val and his guests, until the evening of Fiona's fete.

Spring hung in the breeze, despite the chill, a hint of crushed hyacinths and snowdrops. The carriages had intruded upon a corner of the garden. Penny and her father, disembarking from her father's ancient coach, were met by the creaking sway of the apple trees Appleby was famous for. "What a dreadful noise," her father complained, and Penny could not tell if it was the moaning treetops he referred to, or the scrape of fiddles and the keenness of a pipe trailing from the wide doors of the barn.

They paused to peep in the doorway. The vast, stone-floored apple storage area smelled most pleasantly of the ghost of that ripe fruit, but now, in a flurry of color and movement, it was a Circassian Circle of apple-cheeked young men and woman filled the place. The younger and more energetic of the guests danced themselves warm, eyes bright, laughter on their lips.

She glanced about, wondering if he would be there—hoping.

Her father was greeted by nods.

She did not see him. No Cupid. No Val. No Oscar.

Penny drew her cloak closer against the nip of the wind, against the heated looks from the young men. She ignored them, as the young women ignored her, pretending she was invisible. It never failed to pain her, and yet she expected no more of them. It did not matter, not in the grand scheme of things. Her mother had let things matter too much. Not she. She modeled herself after Lady Anne. She arranged her features in an expression of sublime indifference.

Her father seemed not to notice. She often wondered if her own face took on such a rigid, impassive expression.

"Will you dance, Penny?" one of the Griffith lads asked, eyes bright with hope, the only man in the room gentlemanly enough to ask, and he five years her junior, filled with the confidence of youth.

Was she forbidden fruit to be tasted? Or was it pity she read in his eyes? She considered refusing him. Uncertainty hung uneasy in his lips, his gaze. His eyes spoke of his preparation for refusal—rejection. She saw herself in that look, and took pity.

"Yes," she said. "I am fond of dancing. But it must be later if you do not mind. I would greet the host and hostess of tonight's affair."

He went back to his friends, young lads dressed to the nines. They clustered in a corner and whispered word of her answer with hearty claps upon Griffith's back and shoulders.

He smiled, and said nothing. Not one to gloat, not in front of her. She was glad of that.

Let them dream, she thought. Let them imagine her worse than she was, ready to debauch young lads, prepared to sate their wildest desires, a second Eve of Appleby. None of it was true. She was myth to them, rumor and innuendo. It did not matter. She had promised herself she would dance before the evening was out and enjoy herself doing so. Small matter that the dancer was not to be the one she had imagined.

She and her father stepped out of the warmth and noise into the night, chill and dark. They crossed the tidy farmyard to the house, every window aglow with light, the chimney spouting a plume of warmth.

Fiona opened the door wide for them, releasing the tantalizing odor of baked ham, fresh bread, and apple tarts, laced with the heady perfume and underlying conversational buzz of dozens of guests. She looked like a full-blown apple blossom in a pretty white-and-pink gown.

"Penny! Mr. Foster! Do come in," she cried, catching at Penny's hand as she stepped over the threshold. "You must make a point not to leave early, my friend. A very important announcement is to be made this evening."

"I will not leave until everyone knows of your impending nuptials," Penny promised.

Fiona stared, wide-eyed. "But how do you know? I have not told a soul outside of the family."

"Fiona. Everyone knows Theodore is completely smitten, and must eventually propose. I took the liberty of assuming nothing else could make you quite so happy."

"Oh!" Fiona laughed and gleefully gave Penny's hand a squeeze. "I am deliriously happy. I would wish such happiness on every woman."

Penny thought of Cupid.

"I want everyone I know and love to share the moment," Fiona gushed.

"Even me?" Penny said in mock surprise. "There will be those who condemn you for inviting me into polite society."

"Let them." Fiona's smile faded, but only for a moment. Such happiness was not to be overcome, indeed she laughed and said, "There are those who tormented me as a child, calling me fat Fiona and little dumpling, but never you among them. They have all been invited. It never occurred to me to exclude you."

Penny tucked her arm into Fiona's.

"You are good to me. Does Theodore know what a lucky man he is?"

A frown touched Fiona's ample lips. "Will it be awkward, Penny, that I have invited Val? But perhaps a country hop is beneath him now that he has seen the world and moves in fine company."

"Fine company?" Penny laughed. "Who in the village would you call fine company?"

"Why, his friend, Cupid. Son of a viscount, Teddy tells me. Stands to inherit a fortune. And look! Here come our battle-worn heroes now!"

Into the courtyard pulled the Wharton family coach, the windows flashing with faces grown familiar—Valentine formal in buckish pomp, his companions splendid in brushed and polished uniforms.

Cupid, son of a viscount, no mistaking that shock of dark hair. His eyes met hers through the window as the horses drew to a halt. He looked glad to see her.

Penny excused herself as the door swung wide, and withdrew, unwilling to meet in that moment either Valentine Wharton or his "fine" company.

They disembarked swiftly, greeting the plump, beaming Fiona at the door. Alexander kept looking over her shoulder. He kept his how-do-you-dos brief.

From the coach window he had seen Penny Foster, in a blue velvet dress, the purple cloak about her shoulders. He could see her now, just beyond the door, removing that cloak, fair hair pulled high on her head, blue velvet ribbon wound through the curls, fair tendrils clustered at the graceful nape of her neck. Beautiful. Desirable. As much of a mystery as the day they had met.

It bothered him that she walked away, for as much as he enjoyed observing the enticing sway of her backside, he was sure she had seen him, and he did not like to think himself deliberately avoided.

The farmhouse was a crush, guests shoulder to shoulder and hip to hip. Everyone in Cumbria had come. Cheap cologne and cloying toilet water proved at times eye-wateringly overpowering. Not so overwhelming, however, as observing the ripples in Miss Foster's wake.

This was the second time Alexander had watched her progress in public. As on Valentine's day in the square, she created a stir.

Women hunched their backs and turned away whispering, only to transform themselves at his approach, smiling enthusiastically, turning like flowers to the sun. He found it odd, even obscene, for what was he to these females but a stranger just returned from battle, where he had done unspeakable deeds?

The gentlemen present followed Miss Foster's movements with sly sideways glances, or openly lascivious gazes.

It heated his skin to observe unmasked desire in their eyes. It made him wonder if his own regard for her was in any way ungentlemanly. It pained him to observe the rigid set of neck and jaw as she walked this dreadful gantlet head high, her manner infinitely polite, her smile courageous.

He longed to cloak her from such callous welcome, and yet, it occurred to him that his every interaction with her would be closely observed, and most likely subject to misinterpretation. Their every word and gesture would be open to speculation, to gossips' assumptions. His name and reputation were unknown here, hers cast in stone.

How many years had she suffered such welcome? A wonder she had not become completely embittered, encased in a hard, impenetrable shell. Her former wariness at last made some sense to him.

He resolved to meet her with all deference once he had circulated among the other guests. He would treat her with respect and admiration, as she deserved. But not at once, not first among the many. Her Cupid he might be, and yet he must not seem too eager. That would do her more damage than good.

No. He must open the world's eyes slowly. Not a frontal charge he decided, but a surprise assault.

Chapter Ten

She felt safe, unnoticed, perhaps forgotten. The war heroes, whose attentions were in high demand, passed her by, headed for the music and dancing. She was sure they would not surface again for some time. The house, after all, was hot, stuffy, and filled with the elder set. It was to the dancing barn youth and vigor were drawn.

Cupid surprised her, surprised everyone in the drawing room, by appearing again, an eye-catching muscular specimen towering over a sea of gray hair and balding pates, his deep voice stilling the helpful buzz of well-meant advice to the bride-to-be in which Fiona sat swamped.

"Does my hostess care to dance?" he asked.

Such courtesy did not go unnoticed. It won him the approval of many an aging female, and Fiona responded very prettily with a blush, saying that she would indeed love to dance.

They left the room, arm in arm, a rapier sword beside an apple dumpling, and Penny thought herself again gone unnoticed until his return a quarter of an hour later, when, having fetched a flushed and breathless Fiona a cup of punch, he turned, as if it had been his intention all along, and sought Penny out in her corner by the window. He asked with a formal bow, "Miss Foster, do you care to dance?"

Penny wondered if he knew how much attention his

request won them. She wondered when some well-meaning soul would see fit to warn him away.

"Yes, thank you," she said simply, as Lady Anne might have done, and took his arm, knowing they were watched, knowing that there would be speculation of a growing friendship between them, perhaps even more. As she gripped the muscled strength of his arm, she considered what it might be like to fulfill their wildest assumptions with this marksman, her Cupid.

All eyes surreptitiously followed their exit from the room as he parted the sea of them and plucked up her cloak without so much as having to be told which one. He swung its warmth about her shoulders, the weight of his hands, the embrace of the cloak intoxicating, and yet his hands did not linger. He offered no further reason for gossip, no further fodder for daydreams.

Then they were outside, the night's chill cooling heated cheeks and throat. She lifted her face to the stars, to the moon peeping through moving cloud cover. Ah, Lady Anne, she thought, what am I to do with these feelings? with this gentleman so far beyond my touch?

"Velvet suits you," he said.

A compliment, and so long had it been since she received one she did not know what to do with it. "So soft." She ran her hand along the cloak's sleeve.

"Begs touching," he agreed.

A suggestive remark, an unmistakably teasing glint in his eyes, and yet he made no move to put words to action, as others would have. Did he lack desire? Or an awareness of her reputation? Or did the fogged faces at the window make him keep his hands to himself?

She took strange comfort in the woolen warmth and solidity of his arm's support, in his deferent manner, and yet she did not trust him.

"I have heard, sir, that you are not Mr. Shelbourne at all, but Lord Shelbourne," she said mildly.

He laughed. She liked his laugh.

"Gossip," he said. "Rarely gets the story straight, you know."

"Indeed, I do."

"I thought you might." He drew her hand a little deeper into the crook of his arm. In so doing his hand passed over her sleeve, a quick caress of velvet. It might have been an accident, and yet she knew it was not.

He slowed his steps.

"You mistake me for my brother. He is Lord Shelbourne. Anything else you have heard of me that I may set straight?"

His eyes glinted starlight, challenging her, admiring her, and somewhere deep within fearing what she might say next. *Fearing?* What had he to fear, this cockaded marksman?

"It is assumed you stand to inherit a fortune," she said.

Again he laughed, his breath ghostlike in the moonlight. "Regrettably not, unless a plague of some kind should level the field. I am third in line, you see."

"Ah. And thus obliged to make a living on your own."

"Precisely. The military once seemed a sound direction."

"Once? No longer?"

His gaze strayed, but the answer came swiftly. "No."

"And yet, you were successful?"

"Too much so," he said softly, his voice thin as a knife blade.

"What would you do now instead?" she asked.

"Dance," he said simply.

It had been too long since he had danced, carefree, arms and legs and heart engaged in a pace that had nothing to do with marching, stealth, or a race for one's life. He enjoyed dancing with her, a Ninepins Reel, the steps too fast for much conversation. Their eyes spoke to each other. He could not stop looking at her, and she, eyes glowing, cheeks flushed, looked back with steadfast interest. He could not tell what sent his pulse beating faster, the speed of their movements or the heated promise of amethyst eyes.

She liked him. He could see it was so. It gladdened him. He had begun to think himself beyond liking—on occasion—when the worst of what he had done played itself over and over again in his mind.

And yet, he did not linger at her side when the dance was finished. It would not do to seem too interested, too attentive. He bowed before her and said, "A pleasure." Then he turned reluctantly away from her brightness, her beauty, and asked another young lady to dance. He must remember his purpose.

He led a freckled young woman onto the floor, and watched with satisfaction as a blushing young fellow took Penny Foster's arm. He allowed his gaze to meet hers only when appropriate to the ensuing movements of the Cumberland Square.

Such eye contact made his blood race more than the energetic movements of the dance, but he kept it fleeting, sweeter for its very brevity.

He made a point, when the dance ended, of approaching the group of men in which Mr. Foster stood. Investing himself in a half hour of tedious conversation full of indecipherable local references, he managed at last to make slight mention of the child, Felicity.

"What a kindness that you take her in," he said.

A sudden attentiveness marked the group of gathered Cumbrians, as Mr. Foster, a man of few words and steady gaze, said, "It is no trouble."

"A pity for one so young to go fatherless."

The old man nodded. "And motherless, but for my daughter's care."

Nearby conversations stilled.

"My aunt took in an orphaned girl," Alexander said. "A huge responsibility such an undertaking for a single young woman. No children of her own. No husband to help her."

The weather-worn face proved a closed book, no emotion to be read there, only a bright watchfulness in the faded blue eyes. "But a joy. We love the lass," he said.

"As my aunt does her dear Mary. She is a sweet, taking thing." His gaze strayed to the dance floor, to the sweet taking thing this man's daughter was.

Mr. Foster eyed him steadily, as if to divine his purpose.

Alexander smiled, well pleased with their brief exchange.

As for the old man and others who stood listening, they watched Penny dance, and Alexander, watching them watch her, liked to think they began to see her a little differently.

Oscar was among those who overheard this exchange. He made a point of joining Alexander at the cider cask, where he asked quietly, "Is the child not hers then?"

Alexander shrugged. "I've no idea. Nor would I care to speculate, but I wonder if you would be so good as to ask Miss Foster to dance?"

Oscar watched Penny stepping lightly in a reel, cheeks pink with pleasure. He smiled. "Small hardship. She is a pretty wench, and I hear . . ."

Alexander grabbed his friend in what appeared to be a companionable manner, and squeezing Oscar's elbow, bent his head close to say, "Best behavior, if you please. Most polite."

Oscar's brows rose. He wrenched his elbow from Alexander's grip and grinned as he gave it a rub. "Like her, do you?"

"I would put her out of her misery."

Oscar frowned at this, puzzled, but he did not beg explanation, merely set off to do the honors as the music wound to a close.

Alexander surreptitiously watched Penny join the dance as he made his way around the room, endearing himself to the locals. The evening began to look like a success.

Val spoiled it.

He drank too much from the silver whiskey flask he kept always about his person, liberally spiking the already hard cider, and when he was no longer in full possession of wit or good sense, he swaggered across the dance floor to confront Penny Foster.

Alexander was too distant to hear what it was he asked of her, but the negative shake of her head was an unmistakable as Val's reaction. His faintly inebriated voice carried above the screech of the fiddle, above the enthusiastic thump of the dancers' feet.

"Too much, Touch-me-not? Nonsense, I have not yet had enough. Besides, my dear, I thought you liked me best when my head was turned."

His voice turned heads.

One of the fiddlers missed a note.

The dancers slowed.

The moment sped by too fast, like ball and powder once firing mechanism was pulled. No stopping it.

Oh, Lord, Alexander thought. Not again.

Oscar got to Val first, but not soon enough.

"Is she mine?" Val swayed on his feet, gestures expansive.

Oscar linked arms with him and said something in his ear.

"Don't shush me, Oscar." Val tried to throw him off. "This is none of your affair. I would know. Is she mine?"

Coming up behind his inebriated companion, Alexander could see pain writ plain on Penny Foster's lips, in the downward cast of her eyes.

Alexander braced Val's free arm, leaning into the fog of apple-scented whiskey fumes, "This is neither the time nor the—"

"Time?" Val jerked away, face livid, chin belligerent, his equilibrium affected by the whirl of nearby dancers. "Six years!" he shouted.

The fiddlers squealed to a halt. The piper trailed away. The dancers fell still.

"Six years gone. Never . . . never knew she existed."

His words echoed in the dreadful quiet.

Penny's low voice broke the stillness. "And if you had?" She stood defiant, regal as any queen. "If you had known of her existence? Would you have publicly claimed a child conceived out of wedlock, Valentine Wharton? Would you have resigned your commission? Come home from the fighting? Seen her fed, clothed, educated, and loved?"

"She is mine, then?" Val concluded, voice loud, his focus finite.

She responded in the same calm, well-modulated tone. "I did not say that. I merely ask what would have been different had you known the child existed."

A puzzled look furrowed Val's brow.

"And if I were to say yes? What then? What would you do with an illegitimate daughter, Valentine?"

He shook his head, as if he were a bear and she the buzzing bee. "I would . . . I would . . ."

"Expect your parents to look after her while you jaunt across the Continent? Forget that idea. They have already refused her. Perhaps you would send her off to boarding school? Let strangers see to her upbringing? Tell me, would you name her in your will? Would you allow the legitimate children I am sure you will one day father to know she exists?"

Glaring at her, he flung his punch cup across the dance floor, shattering glass, scattering the flock of dancers. Shocked gasps met his violence. Alexander stepped between the two of them, ready to come to blows if Val turned his anger on Penny.

"Slut," Val spat, loud enough that most everyone present might hear him. It was one of his favorite obscenities when he was drunk.

She flinched, but stood her ground, steely-eyed. "You would be pleased, perhaps, to hear me say no, now, would you not? She is not yours?"

Val's only reply in that instant was to curse her most foully, before casting up his accounts in the middle of the dance floor.

Val dozed on the way home, leaning out of the window occasionally to further relieve himself of too much spirits.

Oscar turned to Alexander during one of these bouts and whispered, eyes narrowed, "Never did get a straight answer out of her, did he?"

Alexander shook his head.

"His, isn't she?"

Alexander sighed, shrugged, heart heavy. "I make no assumptions," he said, his mouth very dry, the taste of cider bitter on his tongue.

Chapter Eleven

It dawned sunny and clear the following day, and Alexander knew at first glance through his bedchamber window where he would find her. He could not, of course, be sure which of the fells Miss Foster would walk, but that she must walk them today was a certainty.

And yet, it seemed he would not have a chance to hunt for her. Red-eyed and hangdog, Val slunk early into the breakfast room, a cheerful room with a southern exposure that Val met almost every morning with a scowl and the order to draw the draperies lest he be blinded by the light.

As a result, Alexander made a habit of breakfasting early, before Val rose, for he liked the light that poured like golden honey across the breakfast table.

"God help me," Val grumbled, squinting at Alexander's bowl of porridge. "I would rather die than down anything so disgusting."

"There is plenty to choose from." Alexander waved at the sideboard.

Val groaned, turned up his nose at the sideboard's steaming dishes, threw himself down in a chair, and carefully, as if it were made of fine china, rested his head upon the white linen tablecloth.

Yarrow followed him in and drew the drapes, throwing a cheerless gloom upon the room that Val met with a grunt.

"Coffee?" Alexander asked, pouring a cup.

"Gently!" Val grumbled when he set the saucer on the table beside his head.

"Headache?" Alexander asked.

The deflated shoulders shrugged wrinkles into the tablecloth. "No worse than usual."

Oscar sauntered into the room, whistling. "Damn, but it's dark in here," he complained, flinging open the draperies nearest the food. He clapped hands together at sight of the sideboard. "Mm. Smells good! And I have worked up quite an appetite with all last night's dancing. I am in the mood for coddled eggs and a rasher of bacon. No! Smoked salmon and mushroom toast."

Val made a muffled groan. "What puts you in such a good mood?"

"Oh, I say." Oscar showed no pity as he spooned eggs onto a plate with a rattle of cutlery and china. "You must have a dreadful head on you this morning, old sod, after last night's fracas."

Val spoke into the tablecloth. "I've no memory of it."

"At Fiona's," Oscar obligingly reminded him.

Alexander gave a hint from his coffee cup. "It involved Miss Foster."

Oscar laughed and waved his fork. "Indeed, it was a frightful fracas at Fiona's over the fathering of Miss Foster's Felicity."

Val rolled his eyes without lifting his head. "Funny."

"It wasn't," Alexander said, carrying his coffee to the window. "Rather embarrassing, really."

"I embarrass you?" Val sounded wearily miffed.

"Not me." Oscar snorted. "I am accustomed to your drunken mean-spiritedness."

Val peered at them from beneath the pale, tousled forelock of his hair, the golden boy, used to being excused the morning after.

Alexander considered his words carefully before he

said, "You're a fine fellow when not in your cups, Val."

"And when I am?" Val's eyes half closed, though whether from the pain in his head or their confrontation, Alexander could not tell.

"You ruin what little reputation Miss Foster has left to her," he said sadly. "Cruelly so."

"Touch-me-not? Bah!" Val waved a hand, as if nothing more need be said.

Alexander stared a moment at the winter-browned garden, the leafless trees. He was not prepared to let the matter drop. "You go too far, old friend. I take no pride in your company when you behave so."

Val shrugged, then laid his head back down upon the table. "This from gentlemen who are beholden to my hospitality," he grumbled.

"True, of course." Oscar forked down a mouthful, pointing the tines at Alexander. "Rather ill-mannered to confront our host in his own home."

Alexander abandoned his coffee cup and rose. "Right you are. I overstay my welcome."

"Damn right!" Val growled.

Alexander stood a moment regarding the top of his friend's head. Dust motes danced golden above the sun-touched hair. "Thank you for having me, Val."

"And me. Superb fishing," Oscar said through a mouthful of salmon as he wiped crumbs from his mouth and rose, chair screeching.

"God! Still there, are you?" Val grumbled into his armpit. "Go on. Get out. I shall be glad to see the backs of you, both of you."

Oscar slid an amused look Alexander's way.

"For that," Alexander said gently, "you must lift your head, old friend."

"And open the draperies," Oscar said with a chuckle.

Val's hand rose, a white flag, waving them away.

Chapter Twelve

Alexander packed his things, saddled the gray, and rode with Oscar through the streets of Appleby before the sun was long risen.

"Heading home, are you?" Oscar asked.

"No," Alexander said. "I have yet to go fell walking."

Oscar laughed. "With the man-eating dog?"

Alexander nodded. "You know me. I love a challenge."

"Right, you are. Where will you stay?"

"Local inn. Give Val time to cool off and sober up. Perhaps we can patch things up."

Oscar raised one brow. "Has he ever been sober? In the time that you have known him?"

Alexander shrugged. "No, but I should hate to end it thus."

Oscar plucked at his mustache. "Care to share a room? I've a mind to get in a bit more fishing, but will soon drown in River Tick if I must pay full price for accommodations."

"I hoped you might stay," Alexander said.

"Do you think he might come round? The lad's prime enough when he is not castaway.

Alexander studied the crenelated tower of Caesar's Tower, pale against the trees. "I hope so."

Oscar promised to book them a room at the Black Boy, a backstreet sort of establishment, nothing to strain their purses, following which he might be found along the river, fishing. They would meet again for supper.

Alexander nodded, handed over his kit, and with a wave to his friend, rode the three miles from Appleby to Dufton, headed for the fells at last, for a sight Miss Foster had mentioned, known as the High Cup.

Dufton was a pleasant, white-cottage village surrounded by orchards, grazing cattle, and a church-topped knoll. Squat sandstone edifices edged a tree-lined green dominated by a post and ball-topped watering trough where he stopped the gray. Latin inscribed the stones, a pun, poorly worded.

Leading the gray to the local livery, he took ruck-sack in hand and walked eastward as the stable lad pointed, uphill to Horthwaite, then to Peeping Hill. Behind him the Eden valley grew smaller. Above him clouds threw shadow over the sun. An eagle keened.

This march into spaces uninhabited, gorse-draped foothills swallowing him, swallowing sound, brought a sense of peace unlike even that he had found at Ulls-water. Here was a grimmer, more sterile beauty, fewer signs of life, in the distance the jagged knife's edge of the fells. Here one might think uninterrupted, or not think at all, only climb, one foot after the other, higher and higher.

Had he ever known Val to be sober, truly sober? Was the child his? And Penny Foster's? Was she the slut Val claimed? He could not bring himself to think so. All Alexander knew was that he wanted to see her again, to speak to her, to hold her in his arms.

Then what? Were his intentions honorable? What sort of relationship was the son of a viscount and a young woman who had borne a child out of wedlock destined to be?

He stopped often to look back.

Out of the wide green ribbon of the river the rippled fabric of the Pennines rose abruptly.

How did one open the eyes of others when blind oneself?

Below him, in a cleft, four white-faced sheep bleated. Herdiwicks. The area was known for them.

The past unfolded in his memory again, the white faces of the young men below, as one of them dropped to his knees, wine red staining the lapel of his uniform. Four French Guard, no more than boys, and yet they were the enemy.

He had been careful with his aim, careful to make every shot count. He would not have them suffer. They looked up at the crack of that first shot, startled, easy targets, squinting against the sun. The second man fell before they reacted to the danger. The youth crouched to shoot wildly. He winged a nearby boulder.

The older man had run.

His own shot did not go wide. The youth looked down, bewildered, fingering the bloody spot, unwilling to believe he was done for despite his show of courage. He fell facedown, pistol cradled in his arm.

Alexander watched the old man who ran while he reloaded, the barrel hot in his hands as he thrust the wad home. He considered letting the coward live, but then the carbine was tight against his shoulder. His orders were clear. The enemy must be stopped—halted in midstride.

Lambs to the slaughter.

Cupid. The men had dubbed him Cupid thereafter.

"How did you manage it?" he had been asked as the bodies were examined. "Clean shots, all of them, right through the heart."

Awe in Val's voice. Gleeful admiration.

How had he managed to do it? Time and again? No glee. No pride did he take in the accomplishment, only a growing weight of sadness, of personal accountability for the taking of lives.

I would not let them suffer. The voice inside his head tried to justify his actions. *I could not.*

Never again, God. Never again shall I pick up a gun to slay my fellow man. This thing I do most solemnly and reverently vow.

A distant rattle of bells, and the sheep below ran—dirty white cotton against the rusted green of the hillside. He turned his face to the peaks again with the feeling that here, so close to heaven, he was heard. He must climb higher, though, must mount what was known as the Beacon to reach the High Cup, the stable lad had said.

Like the empty feeling that came with his memories, the cup opened up before him, a bowl-shaped abyss, massive, symmetrical, littered with boulders. The uneven lip was basalt, steep and craggy—cracked.

He stopped at a rivulet of water named Hannah's Well, wet his handkerchief, and mopped his neck and brow. Not the exertions of the day made him sweat, but those of the past.

There rose within him a need to shout in this place with none but God to hear. And so he threw back his head and cried out like a man possessed. "Forgive me!"

Give me, give me, bounced back at him, no answer but the faint howling of the wind through the rocks above, and the cawing of a pair of startled crows.

The birds took wing with raucous cries, a flutter of pipits exploding from a bank of winter-browned parsley fern.

Penny leaned against the cold rock, heart beating fast. *That cry!* It could be none other. *Cupid! Her Cupid!*

All day she had thought of him, of the kindness he had demonstrated at Fiona's. She had imagined him here, talking to her in firm but gentle voice, comforting her, looking at her with troubled eyes.

Was this cry for forgiveness meant for her? Did he know she waited? Wept?

A clatter of sliding rock meant he stood somewhere below the obelisk, her seat with God and Lady Anne. They often held private discourse here. She leaned over the edge and caught sight of dark hair, thick as broom bristle, the beak of his nose protruding. She could not simply let him walk by.

"Up here!"

He looked up, the sun in his eyes, a streak of moisture on his cheek. "Miss Foster."

For the first time since she had met him, he seemed awkward in raising his hand to shield his eyes.

"You heard?" he asked.

"I should think God Himself heard."

He dropped his hand, dropped his gaze. Not her forgiveness he begged.

And yet she deliberately fostered that mistaken assumption, to put him at ease. "You've no need to ask my forgiveness," she said. "It is Val should be here, on his knees."

He smiled, unbending a little, squinting up again. "Small chance of that. He can barely lift his head today."

She nodded, understanding at once. "What brings you so far from Appleby?" she asked, unprepared for his answer.

"I hoped to find you," he replied.

Chapter Thirteen

Cupid—she had to admit she still thought of him as such—scrambled up the staggered sandstone sides of the jutting rock formation to join her. When he squeezed into the crevice where she rested, she had to slide sideways to allow him room, so small was the space she had chosen. His hip settled dangerously next to hers. Their shoulders bumped provocatively. The muscle of his thigh flexed, and she felt it—how she felt it—from hip to toes.

Heat bloomed in her chest, rising to her cheeks, sinking to the apex of her nether regions. She longed for the flexing of his muscles again.

Lady Anne, Lady Anne, what do I do now?

"A Dufton cobbler, name of Nichol . . ." She addressed her lap, afraid of the look in his eyes, afraid of his closeness, most afraid of her own sense of longing. ". . . climbed up here one day with his bag of tools . . ."

She risked a glance. He smiled, as if he read her mind.

She faltered. "Ah . . . and a pair of boots, which he reheeled while he sat enjoying . . ."

He leaned closer, blocking the wind. "The fine scenery?"

She nodded, unable to look away once their eyes met, warmer now that he was here, warmer in a way that hummed with anxiety and a very unfamiliar sense of anticipation—of potential. "Thus it is called . . ."

"Nichol's chair?" he suggested, eyes full of mischief, a smile tugging his lips.

Oh, Lady Anne! He had already heard the story, and yet he had not stopped her tale, just as she did not stop him when he leaned closer, to kiss her.

Lady Anne forgive her, she kissed him back, and enjoyed the sweet, breath-catching surrender of it, the dizzying, heated intoxication of lips, hands, and breath, until those hands began to stray, first to the small of her back, then lower still, to the curve of her hips, and his lips parted hers to the wonder of his tongue, and a desperate, sweet greediness for more flooded her unlike anything she had ever before experienced.

Remembering herself, of what he must think her capable, she pushed away, saying, "You forget yourself, sir."

"Do I?" A painted look ghosted through his steady gaze.

"I know I do," she said.

The heat in his eyes cooled. "You do not find my kisses to your liking?"

She shook her head and stared at her hands. They seemed so calm folded in her lap. "I have never . . ." The words caught in her throat. "Never liked anything better," she said.

She dared look at him then, and took a deep fortifying breath, that she might resist the brightened heat of his gaze.

"It is just . . . I would not have you think . . . ill of me," she said.

He laughed. "Do I demonstrate in any way that I think ill of you?"

Her face flushed. "I . . . I would not have you believe . . ."

He waited, desire unveiled in eyes that traveled every inch of her face with flattering interest. The corners of his mouth tilted upward. His tongue moistened his lower lip. His breath as he exhaled faintly warmed her cheek.

"The worst of what everyone else believes me capable," she said softly, afraid he might hurt her with just such beliefs.

"Dreadful scene, last night," he said, brushing a strand of hair out of her eyes.

She looked away, remembering, humiliated, his touch unsettling.

"Val is ever at his worst when he has been drinking," he said.

It pained her that he attempted to excuse his friend's behavior.

"He always drowned himself in the bottle after a battle," he went on.

She felt compelled to add, "He drank too much before he went away."

"Did he?" He seemed surprised. "I always assumed—"

"A dangerous thing," she said, cutting him short.

He cocked his head quizzically.

"Assumptions," she said.

She rose, clutching the rough support of cold sandstone, careful not to brush against his leg or his arm. Her knees felt weak, made of aspic. The blood thrummed in her veins.

"Don't go," he begged, catching her hand.

She did not break away immediately, weak to his touch, susceptible to his beseeching look. *Lady Anne give me strength!*

"Do you think Felicity is mine?" she asked.

He was not quick to answer, and yet his opinion lurked in his gaze. Pity there.

She shook him off, crestfallen.

"Whose is she?" he asked.

She was tempted to tell, if only to change the way he looked at her. The secret, the past, ached for release.

"Will you not tell me?"

"I cannot." She concentrated on the placement of her hands and feet, beginning the descent along the rock face.

"Why?" he called after her.

Danger here, she thought—in falling, in trusting. He was Val's friend. She must not forget. Kisses did not change that.

"Talk to me," he begged, approaching the edge.

A pebble hit her head, loosed from beneath his boot. "Back away!" she admonished.

"Do I get too close to the truth?" he asked.

"Danger there as well," she warned, voice sharp.

She made her way down in thought-filled silence, knowing he meant to follow, determined to be on her way before he could catch up. She could not tell him. The reasons no one knew to date still held true. It would be wisest to distance herself from him, from his roving hands and all too tempting lips. She might reveal too much and regret it.

And so she set briskly off up the rise of the Cup as soon as her feet hit the ground, murmuring, "Lady Anne, help me," deaf to his cries of "Wait! Please, wait."

He fell.

Not a long fall, nothing broken, but his knee was badly skinned, his wrists as well, and when he tried to rise, he winced and sank back down with an oath. Tenderness troubled his ankle every time he moved it.

"Damn!"

Miss Foster might help if he could only convince her to turn around, but he hated to beg. He tried to rise, regretted the attempt as pain shot through his ankle, and sank back down again with a groan. What he really needed was some sort of crutch.

Gritting his teeth, he untied his neck cloth, then attempted to remove his boot.

The pain was considerable. He stopped and closed his eyes, debating the best course of action. Did it make sense after all, to remove the boot?

He must beg Miss Foster to return.

He looked up at the sound of footsteps clattering on stone, relieved to find her on her way back.

Out of breath, she stopped, towering over him, her breast rising and falling in a most provocative manner.

"Broken something?" she gasped, her tone full of fear and sympathy.

He shook his head. "I think it is only a sprain. No way of knowing without getting the boot off, and I do not think it will go back on once it is off."

"Swelling?"

"Yes."

"Shall I bind the ankle outside the boot, then?"

"Immobilize it? Kind of you to offer."

She sat down before him, no matter that it muddied her skirt, no matter that she had been bound and determined to separate herself from him a quarter of an hour ago. Cradling his boot heel in her lap, she carefully bound the ankle.

He watched her as she worked, distracted by the curls escaping her bonnet's edge, by the sensation of her hands on his leg, by the potential intimacies of the lap his boot heel so casually plumbed. "Thank you for returning," he said.

"But of course." She looked up. "Why did you not call out for me?"

He shrugged. "Military training. One must do for oneself. How did you know I was hurt?"

She held his gaze a moment. "I happened to look back," she admitted, focusing on his foot again, color rising in her cheeks.

He could not stop a smile, enjoying the idea that she had felt compunction to look back.

Finished with the knot, she gave his boot tip a pat. "There. Best I can do. A pity neither of us brought a walking stick." She rose, hand out for grabbing. "You will have to lean on me."

He clasped the firm strength of her hand and rose, testing his weight on the ankle, for the moment not at all displeased with the absence of walking sticks.

"Much better," he said, anticipating his temporary dependence on her support. "As good as any field surgeon. And now, with your permission." He held out his arm.

She had to step into the curve of it, into what amounted to an unavoidable embrace. She allowed him to drape his arm across her shoulders, to brace his waist with her arm. Her cheeks fired scarlet. She refused to turn and look at him.

He relished the contact, a trifle amused by her discomfort. Hc did not hesitate to settle the length of himself against her. "There. My pretty crutch," he said dryly. "Let's give it a try."

He smelled of sandalwood, and wet wool, and the kisses they had shared. With his arm about her, she could not help but think of those kisses, and when he turned on occasion to look at her, to speak, she got the feeling he remembered them, as well.

Their progress was necessarily slow, and far more intimate than she had anticipated. Their bodies must move as one, a rhythm established between them not unlike that in a three-legged race.

They made adjustments, her hand shifting, grasping his waist more firmly, the pit of his arm settling more firmly against her shoulder. Like puzzle pieces, they interlocked. Their hips and thighs came together for better balance. Unsettling, such contact.

Laughing nervously, they struggled to match their gait, awkwardness bonding them, her heartbeat racing. Eventually, they hit a bumping, jolting stride, now comfortable, and in that level of comfort closer, more intimate. She actually allowed herself to look into his eyes on occasion, into warmth and appreciation and pained amusement.

"Think we will be able to hobble back to the village before nightfall?" he asked.

"We must. You shall have to marry me, else."

"Or set you up as my mistress." He winced.

"Does the thought pain you?" she asked, pained by the suggestion that he would not care to offer marriage.

He laughed. "The ankle pains me."

"You would make me an offer, then?"

He laughed again, as she had intended he should, his chest moving against her rib cage. Then he looked at her, his cheek very close, mischief in his eyes. "I would know more of you if we are to be bound to each other in any way more intimate than we already are."

Again the suggestion that it was not marriage he considered. She kept her eyes on the path, kept her voice steady, and yet there was a thickness to the way the words came out. "What would you know?"

"Everything." The heat of his breath at her ear left her knees weak.

Dear Lady Anne.

She stopped and adjusted her hold on his waist before setting off again. "Surely you jest. A man cannot know everything of any woman."

"True, he can but attempt to unveil the mystery. Care to uncover something of yourself, Penny?"

That he called her by her given name added even more intimacy to a moment already unsettling in its closeness. She could not look at him, did not dare. "There is little to tell," she said, watching the movement of his legs, so close to her skirts, lost in them when the wind blew. "I live a very mundane life. Not full of danger and adventure as yours must have been."

"A life I choose to forget for now. I would be pleased to hear of the mundane."

"It is painful, then?"

"The foot? Not too bad."

"No." She turned her head, daring a glance despite their close proximity. "Remembering."

He said nothing for several strides, his turn to look away, and in the silence she tried to imagine him with gun in hand, shooting.

"I was lucky," he murmured at last. "I survived. Now I would hear of the living. Is she Val's?"

Penny caught her breath, injured again by his low opinion of her. She drew on the strength of Lady Anne, as she always did in such moments. "And if I said she was," she said bitterly, "would you tell him?"

He did not want to imagine the two of them together, Val and this young woman, locked in carnal knowledge, swept away by passion, and yet the image rose unbidden.

"If he is the father, should he not know?" he asked, pulling away so that his hip and thigh no longer pressed hers. A foolish move. It left him suddenly unsteady on his pins, bereft of her support, though he still depended upon her shoulder.

"I am afraid," she said, her words so soft he leaned closer to hear, settling once more against her hip.

"Why? He is not all bad. Assuming the responsibilities of fatherhood might be the making of Val."

"He would take her from me," she whispered.

A peregrine falcon floated on the wind above, keening—a lonely sound. The bird's shadow drifted over them, over the rock-strewn path they navigated with care.

Would Val take the child? he wondered. Would he even want her?

"It must be difficult for you," he said gently, "living with that fear."

Her head snapped in his direction.

"In battle I found it best to face fear head-on. Perhaps it is time you told him."

Her eyes smoldered with angry intensity. For the first time he regretted how closely she was bound to him.

"You've no idea what you're talking about," she snapped.

Chapter Fourteen

She said nothing more, but her whole body spoke stiffly of angry rejection.

"Might we take a moment's rest?" he asked.

She nodded, even seemed glad to shed him. He sat where she led him, raised his foot on a slab of rock that it might throb less, and said, "I regret my presumption."

She stood silently staring back the way they had come, the wind spreading the folds of her cloak about her like dark, velvet wings, the edge of her bonnet guarding her expression.

He tried again. "You are quite right. I've no idea what you . . . your life is like, what might happen if you did tell Val."

She sighed, raised her hand to her neck, and rubbed the nape of it. His weight on her shoulders had taken its toll.

"I am too heavy?" he asked.

She shrugged. Still the treasure of her gaze was kept from him.

"Come." He beckoned.

Had she been a dog, her hackles would have been raised, and yet she turned, first to look at him, then to obey.

"Sit here." He shifted his injured foot to one side on the slab of basalt.

"Why?" She stood, all resistance, her cheeks pinched by the wind, her eyes—he must tell her at a

more appropriate moment how incredible he considered those amethyst eyes.

"I will take that kink out of your neck," he said.

She considered him a moment, suspicion in her
gaze.

He kept his expression carefully neutral.

Hesitantly she sat.

He put gloved hands upon her shoulders.

At once she stiffened.

"Relax," he said. "My batman used to do this at
the end of a long day, when my neck and shoulders
ached most abominably."

"From shooting?"

He had not meant to speak to her of shooting.
"Yes," he said, voice low as he removed his gloves
and rubbed his hands together, then blew on them to
warm cold flesh.

He pulled back the collar of her cloak and lifted a
lock of hair out of his way, and though she shrank
from his touch, he persisted, fingers seeking the heat
of her neck, the tensed joining of neck and shoulder.

Gently, he kneaded the muscle.

"Ow!" she cried, "that hurts!" and might have
pulled away, had he not stopped her.

"It may pinch a bit to begin with, but it gets better.
I promise."

He tried a fresh spot, using both hands on both
sides of her neck, the odor of jasmine rising from her
hair, his eyes closing as he leaned closer, drinking her
in, feeling his way.

"Mm!" She gave a surprised moan. Her shoulders
sank a little, less resistant, and he knew he had hit a
sweet spot.

He smiled, pleased.

"Was it a difficult thing to learn?" she asked.

"No. I just paid attention to what my batman . . ."

She halfway turned, the muscles of her neck con-
tracting, the straw bonnet swiveling, one smooth cheek

exposed, her lips too soft for the words. "I mean the killing."

Odd juxtaposition, he thought, the sensation of her muscles loosening beneath his hands, while his mind tightened around memories he would rather forget.

"A dreadful business." He straightened her shoulders so that her head must turn, the bonnet a welcome barrier between them. He could not bear it should she look at him in that instant. "One shoots rather than be shot, and trusts . . ."

Her neck arched into his hand. She uttered another surprised little moan.

In the touch of his hands on her shoulders, his mind drifted—in the delicate curl of her hair at the nape of her neck, in the slow rise and fall of her breasts as she took breath. He trusted in these implicitly.

What he said was, "In the idea that there is too much living yet to do—to die."

He leaned forward to smell her hair, eyes closing, voice soft.

She turned her head. The silk of her cheek brushed his knuckles, shocking his eyes open.

"There were mornings when I hated to see the sun rise . . ." he said.

She shuddered beneath his hands. He knew not if words or touch stirred her, only that she pulled away with a sigh.

She rose, stretching, her hands first pressed to the small of her back, then rising to touch her neck where his hands had been. "Feels much better," she said. "Thank you."

"Least I can do, seeing as I am the cause."

He accepted her assistance in rising, and carefully, an almost overwhelming level of desire swelling in his chest, he slid the weight of his arm onto her shoulders again.

She turned her head as they set off, her bonnet scraping his ear, her breath briefly warming his chin—

he might have kissed her had she not said in that instant, "She is Val's."

The words struck him like unexpected gunshot. He staggered, and might have fallen.

"Ah!" His own sense of stunned disappointment surprised him as she pressed him more firmly to her, steadying him.

"I suppose I must tell him as much eventually," she said quietly into the curve of his neck.

The smell of jasmine seemed suddenly too sweet.

Betrayed. He felt betrayed.

Chapter Fifteen

A carter hailed them on the road, offering them a
ride. He volunteered to deliver them either to the
apothecary, or the barber of Dufton if they preferred.

"The latter serves quite ably as local tooth extrac-
tor, bone setter, and surgeon," Penny explained.

"Indeed, he does." The well-muscled fellow jovially
boosted Alexander into the back of the wagon amidst
a load of baled woolens, and offered Penny a seat
beside him on the bench with a friendly wink.

As the horses were set into rumbling motion to the
tune of his whistling, Penny flexed the throbbing arm
with which she had braced her Cupid's waist, and
threw a glance over the shoulder he had taken time
to rub the soreness from. "You all right back there?"

Hip and thigh still tingled with memory of his
body's movement against hers.

"Fine," he replied. "Enormously glad to get off
that foot."

He sounded polite, his look her way no more than
a glance, as if nothing had happened between them,
as if she had said nothing of importance.

What had possessed her? Why trust this stranger,
Val's friend, with a secret so powerful he might de-
stroy her with it?

She shivered, clutching her cloak tight. How cold
the wind blew against the shoulder Mr. Shelbourne
had warmed, almost as cold as his reaction to her
revelation that Felicity was Val's.

She should have held her tongue. *Dear Lord*, she should have held her tongue.

Penny held the door wide for him with a jingle of the overhead bell, a cheerful announcement of their weary little party. Alexander tried not to wince as he leaned into the carter's arm and hopped over the threshold.

Penny shut the door behind him. The narrow shop seemed suddenly very crowded and rather darker than before, for the three of them blocked the window's light.

The barber of Dufton looked up from the man he stood shaving, and bade his reclining customer, "Please vacate the chair, Mr. White. The gentleman's injuries take precedence."

Mr. White, who bore the distinction of wearing nothing but black, in direct contradiction to his name, swiveled his newly trimmed head to get a look at the intruders, his pale, lantern jaw half shaven, a look of discontent turning down the corners of a purse-pinched mouth.

"Not at all," Alexander insisted, though the ankle throbbed horribly, and he longed for relief. "No more than a sprain, this. If you will be so good as to help me to the bench, I will wait my turn."

The carter saw nothing unusual in his request, and obligingly helped him to the bench, but Penny frowned as he sank down with a wince.

"Well, Miss Foster," the barber said as he tilted his customer's head and applied the blade with a practiced rasping sweep. "Do you bring me another injured stray?"

Penny's frown grew more pronounced. Alexander wondered if she meant to insist the barber attend to him at once. "Mr. Shelbourne is a guest of Valentine Wharton's, Mr. Bridgeman," she said briskly. "Newly returned from fighting on the Continent. Can you not—"

"Ironic, really," Alexander interrupted with a laugh. "Napoleon gave me nary a scratch, sir, but I have fallen on your fells."

Both Mr. Bridgeman and Mr. White had a dry chuckle at that.

Miss Foster regarded them all impatiently. "Perhaps you have something to dull the gentleman's pain while he waits, Mr. Bridgeman?"

"Are you in pain, Mr. Shelbourne?" Bridgeman was anxious to please. "I've rum," he said. "But the lad must run to the gallipot if it's opiates you want."

"No need for that," Alexander protested, too late. Miss Foster was already out the jingling door again with a hasty "I'll go."

The three watched her determined departure. She was a sight worthy of admiration, the wind kicking her cloak as she went, catching at her hair, whipping color into alabaster cheeks. A stirring sight, this beautiful young woman, and all her concern for him.

"You could not be in better hands, sir." Bridgeman's razor swept clean Mr. White's soap-lathered chin with a final stroke. "Miss Foster is always taking in the broken and injured. Dogs, cats, wild ponies. Ain't that right, Mr. White?'

He rocked back on the balls of his feet to tap the blade clean against the brass bowl held tight to Mr. White's neck.

His pale customer fingered freshly shaven skin and looked about him, as if he had something important to tell.

"Took in Eve of Appleby, didn't she?" he asked, his voice lowered to a conspiratorial murmur. "And her blow-by."

Barber and customer looked at each other by way of the mirror and nodded, as if at a profound truth.

Who?

"More than her family would do." The barber's neatly trimmed brows rose. His thick lips pursed contemptuously.

A lad appeared from the back of the shop, silencing them. He bore a wooden tray, and on it a sweating canister. Bridgeman lifted the lid with tongs, steam belching forth, and bade the lad, "Back to the wig washing."

Mr. White said, "Whatever became of the child?"

Bridgeman delved into the fog with the tongs, lifting a strip of smoke-wrapped linen, silencing White's questions with hot toweling.

"Joy, they named her, was it not?" His brow furrowed. "I'll never know why. Nothing in the least joyful in that poor child's birth."

Alexander nodded, as indication of his interest, his ankle forgotten. "Who was Eve of Appleby?" He could not stop himself from inquiring.

The two men exchanged a look. Mr. White plucked the toweling from his mouth as if he could not hold back his response.

"Local strumpet," he said.

"Comely lass." Bridgeman nodded as he took the damp toweling from White and applied a little horsehair whisk broom to the man's neck cloth. "A pity I could not save her. Died bearing the child." He shook his head sadly.

Mr. White examined his freshly shaven jowls in a pewter-backed mirror as he rose from the barber's chair. He handed Bridgeman a coin, then turned to Alexander. "The chair is yours, sir. I do thank you for waiting so patiently. It is not often a man of my profession receives such a courtesy."

Bridgeman nodded, dusting hair off the barber's chair with a snap of linen toweling.

"And what occupation might that be?" Alexander asked, intrigued.

"My card," White said, and handed him an elaborately engraved bit of pasteboard, the edge banded in black.

"Will you take my arm in rising?" The barber offered Alexander his elbow.

"Perhaps if we brace him both sides?" Mr. White offered.

"How very kind of you." Alexander took advantage of their arms, the barber's and the undertaker's. A fortunate encounter, he thought—one might almost say felicitous.

She returned from the apothecary, a packet of white powder in hand, instructions for mixing of same with water scribbled on the side.

All Alexander could think when he spied her through the window was that this kind soul allowed the world to think her a fallen woman for the sake of a strumpet named Eve, and he did not understand why.

Mr. Bridgeman knelt before him, cutting the boot away, and none too gently. He gripped the arms of the barber's chair, lips pressed tight, stoically bearing the man's clumsiness.

He closed his eyes and clamped his jaw against the threat of a most unmanly yelp as the bell announced her return. Bridgeman, distracted, turned to see who it was, momentarily relaxing the pressure on his ankle. Alexander managed a smile for Miss Foster. She responded with answering warmth, her gaze almost as probing as Bridgeman's fingers as they resumed the destruction of his boot.

Alexander gritted his teeth and gripped the arms of the chair once more, smile fading, his eyes closing involuntarily.

"Mr. Bridgeman," she said sharply.

"One moment, Miss Foster." The barber waved her away.

"No, sir," she said firmly. "Now, if you please."

Bridgeman stopped sawing the dearly bought

leather. Hoby made a stout boot to military specification if one was willing to pay the price.

Alexander unclenched his jaw.

"The boot must come off." Bridgeman waved the instrument of destruction. "The swifter the better. His foot is horribly swollen."

"And more easily so, would you not agree, if you know you do not pain him in the extraction?" she asked.

The barber could not argue the point, and yet he tried.

"Pain, my dear? He does not complain. Do I add to your injuries, sir?"

Alexander almost pitied the fellow.

Miss Foster muttered something under her breath. He thought it sounded like a name, repeated twice. *Lady Anne?* Then she put a hand on the barber's shoulder before he could commence torturing his Hessians. "He is a soldier, sir," she said, her voice low. "What do you expect him to say?"

Bridgeman eyed her, then him, thinking.

"I shall have to probe for broken bones. Perhaps it would be best." Rising, he rang for a pitcher of cool water.

Alexander watched Miss Foster measure powder into a glass. She had pretty wrists, a pretty way of moving. More beautiful than these was the look of concern in her amethyst eyes. Concern for him.

Who was Lady Anne, and why did the name sound vaguely familiar?

"Thank you, Penny," he said when she handed him the powder-clouded glass.

She froze, her gaze meeting his. Perhaps her hand trembled a little. Certainly the surface of the water danced as he took the glass, their fingertips brushing.

She let go, lashes fanning down over her magnificent eyes. "I do not like to see anyone suffer needlessly, sir," she said softly.

He paused, his lips hovering above the brim of the glass, eyeing her keenly, her words more significant to him than she could know. He had used those same words, almost exactly those words when Oscar had taken him aside one day and asked, "Why the heart, Cupid? Always the heart?"

He wondered if she would understand that he had not liked to see any man suffer, even in the killing of him.

Miss Foster's gaze had risen to his face again. She waited for her potion to be drunk. Would she consider him worthy of her mercy if she knew the things he had done?

He tossed back the tincture in a single gulp, wincing at the taste. Handing her the empty glass, he faced Bridgeman, gripped the chair again, and said lightly, "I am at your mercy, sir."

"I think you are right," Bridgeman said at last, when his patient sat ashen and panting, clutching the chair as if it might walk away while he briskly rebound the foot. "Nothing but a nasty sprain. Must stay off of it as much as possible, young sir. You will need tending. Do you stay at Wharton Hall?"

"Yes," Penny blurted when it took Cupid some time to unclench his jaw and say in exactly the same moment, "No."

"What?"

The packet of powder seemed now to take effect, for Alexander Shelbourne laughed, sleepy-eyed, almost giddy in saying, "Val kicked us out this morning."

"Why?" Penny asked.

Shelbourne stared blankly a moment, as though he could not quite remember. "Oh, yes!" He smiled. "Dared to question his honor, we did, when he suffered the headache. Unwise, that."

"But where will you stay?"

"Ought to go home," he said. "Must face them eventually."

"You cannot travel so far with this injured foot."

He shrugged. "Oscar will look after me."

"And where is Oscar?"

"Inn . . ." he said, eyelids drooping, head beginning to bob.

"In what?" she said.

"Black Boy," he murmured as he drifted off to sleep.

When the wagon stopped jiggling and jerking over the uneven road, the sun was setting. The golden glow of it met his squinting attempts to open his eyes, warm against his face, too bright in his eyes. Groggy, he felt, heavy and stupid and groggy.

He heard her tell the pony whoa, heard a dog bark, and then her father's voice.

"What's this, then?"

"Mr. Shelbourne," she said. "Fell from Nichol's Chair."

"Is he killed?"

Alexander wanted to laugh and longed to say, "No. The barber of Dufton did that," but his mouth wouldn't work. His throat rasped the words in an inaudible murmur that sounded like a breathless grunt.

"You bring him here?" Penny's father sounded annoyed. "I do not think it wise, my dear."

"I know," she agreed. "But he and Val have had a falling out, and the inn he mentioned staying at with his friend Oscar has no record of either of them."

"Give me the reins," her father ordered gruffly. "I will drive him to Wharton's."

Again he tried to speak with no more luck than before, limbs leaden, tongue too thick.

Her voice again, sweet in his ears. "You surprise me, Father. Would you turn away someone in need?"

Penny. Sweet Penny. She played Samaritan for him.

"Perhaps I should have." Her father's voice was subdued. "I should have more carefully guarded your reputation, Penny, my love."

She laughed. "How? Would you have turned Eve away?"

Eve again. He tried to sit up, to pay attention.

"Would you have risked Felicity to another's kindness?"

No response to that. A horse nickered. The wagon creaked and shook beneath him as she stepped down.

"There is no turning back the clock, Father."

"I should have—"

"What? Ruined the girl's chances, to save mine? Nonsense. Never mind that. What are your wishes now, with regard to poor Mr. Shelbourne?"

Her voice was louder now. She stood at the tailgate of the wagon.

Her father's sigh was one of resignation. "Call Weaver and Tom, lass. We'll never manage carrying him in on our own."

He lay upon the bed beside her chair, slack-jawed, his eyes closed, foot raised, an occasional moan slipping lips gone soft with sleep.

Not a pretty fellow, her Cupid, and yet sight of him stirred her. He filled the bed to overflowing, so tall his feet dangled off the end, so broad-shouldered that she, who had always considered herself a strong, big-boned lass, felt quite small beside him.

Strong, weather-tanned hands rested dark against the linens—hands that knew well how to handle a gun—hands that had killed.

His hair spilled wantonly upon her pillow. Penny's fingers itched to touch the bristling thickness, to skim the stubble-darkened chin. She stroked Artemis's ears instead, unable to stop looking at Alexander Shelbourne's mouth, remembering how he had kissed her at Aira Force—a breathtaking kiss—a breathtaking look in his eyes.

With a sigh she delved her fingers deep in Artemis's neck ruff, imagining what might have been, what might still occur.

Artemis rested her head upon her knee, her loving golden brown gaze riveted on her face.

Sweet daydreams. She passed the tip of her tongue along her lower lip. She had almost forgotten how soft, how warm and demanding a man's mouth might be. As Val's had once been.

Penny's hand fell still on the dog's neck. She considered kissing this rugged Cupid as he lay sleeping. The urge to do so welled far more strongly than she imagined possible.

She pressed her lips together, stifling desire.

Tears needled the backs of her eyes. She longed to let the tears spill down her cheeks, years of regret and longing made liquid. *Oh, Lady Anne! Is this what life was like for you?*

With a low whuff, Artemis nudged her hand with the back of her head. She sighed, gave her head another pat, and blinked the tears away. She was not Lady Anne. She was nothing but a tarnished penny, nothing to do about it. Not worth much. Not worth crying over.

Artemis stood, attention shifting to the figure in the bed.

"Hmm?" Her Cupid made a breathy noise, lips moving, eyes rolling beneath closed lids. To her surprise he murmured, "What's so funny?"

Was he awake? His eyes remained closed, his breath deep and even.

She held her breath and said nothing, staring at the fullness of his lower lip, wondering if he talked in his sleep.

The dog yawned and stretched, then ambled toward the door. She heard the thump of her passage as she bounded down the stairs, met by the sound of her father's voice.

Her gaze never left Cupid's face. He would go away. She had seen it in his eyes when she told him Felicity was Val's.

He would go away, and with him her last chance for kisses.

She eased up from her chair, leaning in over him, studying more closely the smooth sheen of his lips, the scattering of pale freckles on his cheeks, the rise and fall of his chest.

Her father would come up soon to see how their guest did.

For the moment she was glad to have him to herself, to wonder what it might be like to have such a man to husband. She had resigned herself to the impossibility of such a future, and yet Lady Anne had married twice. Why not she? With this great wonderful warrior lying prostrate in the guest bed, she allowed herself to imagine it, to fully comprehend what it was she had given up. For Eve. For Felicity. For her mother's sake.

As she leaned in closer to gaze at him, at the darkening stubble upon a jaw gone slack with sleep, at the faintly bluish tinge to his eyelids, at the pink spot on his cheek that bore the impression of wrinkled pillow cover, she mourned the passing of dreams, of a future with children of her own.

He opened his eyes. A flicker of lashes, a flash of emerald, and with a sudden intake of breath, he half rose from the bed, expression alarmed, as if she posed a threat. He had her arms pinned to her sides before she knew what he was about, a wild darkness in his eyes.

"Mr. Shelbourne," she gasped.

He blinked, alarm fading, light blooming in his eyes. He gave his head a shake, then let go his hold on her. "Miss Foster!" He took a deep breath. "Forgive me."

A lovely green, his eyes. Had she read fear in them?

Not of her, but of what he might have done to her?

"Back on the battlefield?" she asked.

He nodded, his gaze sliding away, regret pulling down the corners of his mouth.

He was, in that moment, a stranger again. She caught glimpse of all that lay hidden from her. Her former assumptions of what sort of man he was were dwarfed by reality.

His gaze trailed assessingly about the room.

"I brought you home," she said. "Oscar was not booked at the inn you mentioned."

"You have tried the others?" he asked, his voice ragged.

She blinked, perplexed. "You wish to go?" She allowed no hint of regret to color the words.

A trace of emotion flickered greenly. Was it longing in his eyes?

"Oscar will wonder what's become of me."

His mouth seemed strangely vulnerable, this mouth she might have kissed one last time, had she been braver and bolder.

"I shall send for the carriage at once," she said.

Chapter Sixteen

Alexander tossed the letter upon the unmade bed, and leaning into his cane, hobbled to the closet for his bag. Jamming an armload of gear into his kit, he wished—*Oh Lord,* what could a man wish under such circumstances? That the world made sense, and his purpose in it? That the good and just might be blessed while evil and deceit were vanquished? That children need not suffer?

His thoughts pained him as much as his ankle. He sat on the bed with a sigh.

Oscar looked up from the tiny bundle of silk floss and feathers he was tying by the meager light of the rain-spattered window. "Post coach, is it, then?" He snapped a thread with his teeth.

"Must, much as I shall hate it. Faster than horseback with this blasted leg."

"Do you take the gray?"

"No." Alexander regarded three odd stockings in frustration and wondered where their mates had gone. "Will you send him? Better yet, bring him. Meet my family. I should like them to know you."

Oscar snipped at his feathery bundle with a tiny pair of sewing scissors. Behind him, rain tapped at the window.

"I will not be in the way?"

"Never!" Alexander said in all earnestness. "We've no salmon, but eels, perch, and pike aplenty."

Oscar compared his feathered fly to those clustered

on the brim of the hat on which he displayed more than a dozen. "I just might take you up on that. Little enough reason to keep me here." He looked up. "Any word from . . ."

Alexander hastily shoved a stray neck cloth into the bag and buckled it closed. "Val? No. Though, if he should ask . . ."

Oscar's brows arched.

Alexander stared at the painting on the wall, a hunting dog, a felled dove dangling from its jaws. "He is welcome to come with you and the gray if he should care to mend things."

"You are far too charitable with the fellow, Cupid." Oscar's gaze shifted from fly to window. "Hallo!"

"Is it the coach already?" Alexander stuffed shirts into his second bag with reckless abandon.

"No." Oscar winked mischievously. "A young lady approaches. She who so recently rescued you from your own clumsiness." His merry expression faded. "But what have you done to ruffle her feathers, my friend? Miss Foster looks a wee bit miffed."

Alexander frowned, then hobbled to the window.

She did look miffed. Livid, in fact, skin flushed, her posture rigid with anger as she strode toward them, bonneted head bowed against the rain. No question where she was headed. She looked up now and again to scowl at the inn.

"Haven't the foggiest," Alexander admitted.

Bags packed, the two of them proceeded to the common rooms with as much speed as Alexander could muster, Oscar in the lead, bearing his kit.

The clerk caught sight of them and beckoned.

Amethyst eyes flashing, she turned, rain flung from her cloak and from the brim of her bonnet. "You!" she said, her tone so strident the clerk blinked, and a maid heading up the back stairs paused and ducked her head to watch.

Beside him, Oscar sucked in a breath with a surprised "What've you done now?"

"I trusted you!" she called out in tones that bespoke him anything but trustworthy.

The inn master's wife poked her head out of a backroom. " 'Tis Penny Foster," she whispered to someone over her shoulder.

Behind him a door opened with a muffled "What's all this, then?"

"I trust you'll settle this while I see to buying your passage?" Oscar murmured, plucking at his mustache.

Alexander nodded, gave Oscar's shoulder a squeeze, and leaning heavily into his cane, hobbled toward her, that he might ask quietly, "Is something wrong, Miss Foster?"

"As if you did not know!" Her cheeks flushed a deeper hue. The flash of anger in her eyes confused him.

The desk clerk tried to look busy and disinterested. The inn master's wife vacated the doorway, her husband peeping out in her stead.

"I am at a loss." Alexander shifted his cane and held up his free hand, trying not to wince.

Doubt moved like a shadow across her features. "You told him," she said, low-voiced. "I did not think you could be so cruel."

The desk clerk glanced his way. He caught sight of the movement out of the corner of his eyes, his attention focused on Penny, on the distrust in her eyes.

"I've no idea . . ." he began.

His words fired her anger afresh. "Surely you knew he would take her! She is everything to me, and he . . ." Her voice broke.

"Val?"

She nodded, tears welling, bright as the raindrops dewing her bonnet. "He has taken Felicity."

*   *   *

"Come. Walk with me," he said as he guided her out of the common room, out of the inn entirely, into the wet and miserable coach yard, one hand firm at her elbow, the other clutching his cane—as if together they had somewhere to go.

Angry with him, pained beyond measure, she flung his hand away. "You dare to pretend we are still friends?"

"Are we not?"

"How can you possibly think we would be when it is you who told him, you who succeeded in separating me from the one person in the world I love most."

"You assume I told him."

"Yes!"

"I did not," he claimed, leaning into his cane.

"Liar," she blurted, turning heads all along the gallery that encircled the coach yard, her emotions undone, the accusation too hasty. She wished it unsaid as soon as the word left her mouth.

His jaw stiffened. On he hobbled in silence until she stood ready to blurt out fresh impertinence, and he opened his mouth as if addressing an ill-mannered child. "I am greatly offended you would blame me above all others, that you would assume I betray you in so vile a manner. Val and I have not spoken since the morning you and I . . ." He tapped his bound foot. "Since this happened."

She did not know whether to believe him.

"He said . . ."

She remembered exactly what had been said. The moment had played and replayed itself in her mind. The dog heard him coming, and had risen with a growl, hackles raised.

The hair at the back of Penny's neck had prickled as she stepped through the doorway to the tune of approaching hoofbeats.

"She's mine, isn't she?" he had shouted as the bay clattered into the courtyard.

The dog met him, stiff-legged, teeth bared. The big bay had side-stepped, wall-eyed. Val wrenched on the reins with an oath.

She bade Artemis sit with a gesture and silently called on Lady Anne to guide her.

Val had been drinking, enough that she could smell it on his breath, not enough that it impaired his movements, gaze, or speech.

She wiped flour from her hands onto her apron. She and Felicity had been helping Cook make bread.

"She's mine, and you keep her." He spoke in a more conversational tone, his gaze straying to the child, who stood wordlessly in the doorway.

He eyed her keenly as he stepped down from the horse, a hawk after a rabbit.

Felicity backed away a step.

Penny said nothing, admitted nothing. He knew the answer already.

"You cannot deny her me." His voice rang with authority as his gaze fixed briefly on Artemis growling another throaty rumble, every muscle tensed for attack.

Felicity ran to Penny, tucking herself behind the wall of her skirt, fingers clutching Penny's hand.

"I am your papa, child." Val squatted, smiling, his hand out. "You must come with me."

For a moment, fair hair gleaming in a brief burst of sun, he looked like the Val of her past, a handsome, coaxing, self-confident Val.

"My papa is dead," Felicity objected, her words souring his expression. When he rose, scowling, Felicity clung tighter to Penny's hand, her free hand worrying with the locket she always wore.

Val stepped closer, overshadowing them both. "That necklace, child," he asked brusquely, reaching for it. "Where did you get it?"

Felicity backed away, big-eyed, grasping the heart-shaped bit of gold as if he meant to take it. "My mama wore it the day she died," she said, her voice rising. "It contains a lock of my father's hair."

"And does it not match this?" He grabbed at his own fair locks, tugging the golden strands with a grim sort of desperation.

Felicity frowned. Curls of matching gold bobbed as she turned to face Penny, trust in her eyes.

"It cannot be the same. Can it, Penny? You said he was dead."

Voicing the lie again did not make it so. In the child's earnestness, in Val's baleful glance, Penny found her own shame.

When she did not immediately respond, Felicity repeated defiantly, voice quavering, "You said."

Penny knelt, admitting softly, "I . . . I was wrong."

Trust died in the child's eyes in an unmistakable progression of shock and pain. She stepped back, bewildered.

Penny wanted to weep.

"And Mama?" Felicity's voice had gone high and thin.

Oh God! Lady Anne. What have I done?

Val took advantage of her silence. He swept Felicity into his arms. "There, there now, child. Don't fret. Papa is here."

He walked with her toward his horse.

She did not fight him.

Artemis growled once more. For the veriest instant, Penny considered siccing the dog on him, for in that instant, heart sinking, she knew the child was lost to her—lost to the lie with which she had always tried to bind Felicity to her tightest.

She bade the dog stay with shaking voice and followed Val, begging shamelessly, "Leave her, Val. Please. Do not take her away." Her voice broke, the sound of her despair dreadful to her own ears.

Tearful and wide-eyed, Felicity's gaze flitted from

Val's face to hers and back again as he mounted the horse, cradling her to his chest.

"Penny?" she cried uncertainly, little hands reaching, little arms stretched wide. "I don't want to go."

"Please, Val, I beg you." *Lady Anne help me!*

Jaw rigid, without another word Val had gigged the bay, Felicity weeping, her cries of "Penny!" tossed on the wind, lost in the drum of hoofbeats.

The sound of hoofbeats, of wheels on cobblestone, and Oscar's muffled shout of "Post coach is come!" roused Penny from her verbal reverie.

Her gaze rose from Mr. Shelbourne's cane to meet the very real concern in green eyes grown familiar as he took her gloved hands in his.

"I wish I could help," he said.

He wished?

She fell back, stunned, his grip on her fingers a deceit, and yet she must ask, must know. "Will you not speak to Val? Convince him she must stay with me?"

Passengers disembarked in a small flood behind him. He looked over his shoulder.

Oscar handed the coachman coin.

He was leaving. She could see it in his eyes. He meant to abandon her. *No. No. Lady Anne, not again!*

"Will you not go to him? Plead her return?" Desperation in her voice. She hated to hear it.

The coachman cried out for passengers as fresh horses were led into the traces.

She pulled her hands from his. "I thought . . ."

Rain dripped from his hat brim, dewing his cheeks. "I . . . I am sorry. I wish . . ." His eyes, dark as storm clouds, begged forgiveness. "Forgive me. I must go."

Oscar helped him to board, murmuring something about the gray, and all the while his gaze, stricken, followed her as she backed away, more heartbroken than before, more alone than she had ever been, cheeks wet, but not with rain.

Chapter Seventeen

She wept as she walked home to a house empty but for the maids, her father overseeing his holdings, no Felicity to greet her. The place smelled of last night's mutton, wet leather, and drying wool. Would these walls ever ring with the child's laughter again? Penny wondered, and found them too close for the grand scope of her sadness.

Eyes misting with fresh grief, she escaped the house, walking uphill—Artemis at heel, devotion in her great brown eyes, in the comfort of her jaw on Penny's knee whenever she stopped to rest.

Penny walked into the mists, into the sodden folds of a countryside as bleak and barren and hopeless as her future. She walked until she was exhausted, until she had wept as much as her heart demanded, until she could find no new manner in which to blame, castigate, or rail against her own foolishness. Her clothes were soaked. Her breath formed white clouds. Her heart weighed heavy. The cold air cut her lungs raw. The skies lowered like her mood, damp and cold as the emptiness within.

She strode the heat of her anger out of her system. Sadness remained. And the dog. Artemis stayed beside her, tireless and undemanding.

Fool! She was a fool. Always a fool when it came to men. How could she have told him what had so long been kept safe in secrecy. How could she have allowed Felicity to fall into Val's hands? What could she do to get the child back again? To forget the man who had ruined her life, and broken her heart, this Cupid she had fallen in love with? What would Lady Anne do?

There was no legal recourse. She had no arguable claim on the child. She doubted Val would listen to reason. He had never been a reasonable fellow.

Cupid was gone. He could not get away from her fast enough. She had read the distance in his eyes from the start, and paid no heed. What had made her believe he cared for her? For the child? Why did she persist in believing better of men than they deserved? She would never see him again.

She prayed for a hardening of her heart, that it might not pain her so awfully, that her losses might not leave her so weak. She tried to see the sense of it, the pattern.

The fells, misted gray, offered no answer, only the wind whistling through the rocks, the distant bleating of sheep, and the raw, muddy breath of wet earth.

At the wind-whipped crest of a rocky outcropping that drew her now as never before, she thought of her mother, and contemplated the dizzying leap. Were there answers below? In the silence that would follow?

A fleeting thought, terrible in every way. It left her more spent than before, as if will and hope and perseverance had leapt without her and lay smashed on the rocks.

A high-pitched keening sprang from Artemis's throat. In looking down, she realized the dog's attention lay behind her.

She turned. Her father stood no more than three yards away, wind tugging at his sparse gray hair, his nose beet red, a wisp of smoke drifting from the pipe clenched in yellowed teeth.

"Not thinking of going the way of your mother, are you, lass?"

How haggard his face, she thought.

She stepped away from cliff's edge, away from the pain she stirred in him, standing here on the brink of the past. "No, Father. I've not the courage for such a leap."

"Courage?" Anger lit the embers of his faded blue gaze and fired briefly in the bowl of his pipe. "A coward's way, that." Smoke ghosted from the corners of his mouth. "It takes courage to go on, lass."

Like Lady Anne. She shivered.

"I would not abandon you, Da," she said, chin wobbling, voice uneven.

He opened his arms. She stumbled into them, warm haven, her port in life's storms.

"Thas good, lass," he spoke softly, his voice rumbling in his chest, his hand patting the middle of her back. "I could not bear it, you know."

She nodded, the wool of his coat harsh against her cheek, the smell of tobacco engulfing them.

"I have been to Wharton's," he said.

She looked up, drying her eyes on the back of her glove.

He frowned, his gaze fixed on the horizon. "Wouldna see me," he said, dashing hope. "Wouldna let me so much as lay eyes on the child."

She went herself the following day, and was turned away as brusquely as her father had been, and so to bolster flagging spirits, she went to the great picture at Appleby Castle and looked upon the three faces of Lady Anne, taking some comfort in remembering a long life well lived. As she passed the almshouses Lady Anne had found solace in building, she resolved to begin rebuilding the poor abandoned creature that she, herself, fast became. She could not weep forever. Far better to get on with life, to fight what seemed insurmountable obstacles, to re-create where others had torn asunder.

She went home again, to remind her father that the walls of the pony pen needed expanding. Together they set to work, stone upon stone. A balancing act. Rough work. Strange comfort to be found in the heat and sweat of physical exertion, in fortifying the protection of that which was dear. Penny wore out her anger in building the pen, walling in what strength was left her, fortifying her defenses against the darkness of despair.

Despair had swallowed her mother. She could not give in to it as well. Life went on. Lady Anne had found a better way.

She did not hear him coming. Even Artemis gave little warning, a flurry of barks from the courtyard, and then she fell silent, not the man-eater she was reputed to be when the man brought a fish head for gnawing.

His shadow fell upon her as she worked. For a moment, heart leaping, Penny thought him Cupid, returned. Then he spoke, destroying the fantasy— surprising her. Oscar Hervey, Cupid's friend, not Cupid.

"Miss Foster?"

She raised a gloved hand to shield her eyes. He stood, hat in hand, awkwardly twisting the brim.

"Mr. Hervey?"

"Alexander asked me to check on you."

The words, unexpected, snuck under her defenses. She forced a pleasant tone, picked up another stone, and settled it into place. "Most kind of both of you, I am sure, but Mr. Shelbourne need not concern himself."

"Asked me to check on Felicity as well."

"You have seen her?" Vulnerable again, the words tumbled from her lips.

"No, uhm . . ."

"Oh." She bent to pick up another rock.

"I wondered if you'd care to go with me, to call on Valentine."

She stood there, the rock clutched to her chest. "You would take me?"

"Shelbourne's suggestion. He hated to leave so suddenly."

"Of course." She hardened her heart at mention of him and added to her wall. She would not be foolish again.

"Cares for you, you know?"

She met his declaration with silence, unwilling to believe, to hope, her gloved hands stilled atop the stones.

"I've never seen him so smitten," he persisted.

"Then why . . . ?" She banged her gloves together, watched the dust fly, then bent to fetch up another heavy stone. "He seemed so anxious to go," she said.

Oscar shrugged. "Can't blame him. Fond of his nevvie."

"Nephew?" Her eyes widened. The rock, too heavy, spilled from her grip.

He stepped forward, a look of concern puckering his brow, as if he might step through the very wall to help. "Ill. Thought you knew."

She squatted beside the fallen stone, shaken and confused, unwilling to let him see her emotions. She knew nothing. Gritting her teeth, she took better grip, hefting the stone, and settled it in place with a clatter. "He said nothing of it."

She stood back to examine her progress.

From behind her a low growl sounded. Artemis leaned into her skirt, legs tense, gaze fixed on Oscar. She smelled fishy.

Oscar plucked at his mustache. "Private lad, our Cupid."

Penny slipped a glove to lay hand on the collie's head. "Enough, Artie," she murmured. She relaxed her stance.

"And loyal." Oscar stopped plucking. "Loyal as your dog."

"Indeed?" Swept by an intense feeling of guilty relief, Penny had to admit herself comforted by his words. She stroked the dog's ears. "Assumptions can wreak havoc with one's life, can't they?"

Oscar nodded.

Together, they rode the oak-lined avenue that cut the manor's park in two. Together, they mounted the broad stone steps, to stand on Val's doorstep, the lion's head knocker freshly rapped.

Uneasy, Penny turned to Oscar and said, "I am concerned that this will pain the child."

"How's that?"

"She will have to watch me go away again."

"You do not think it would pain her more to hear nothing from you?"

"Will Val let us in?"

"Quite possibly not. Depends on what he's had for breakfast."

The great oak door opened on the aging butler, Mr. Yarrow, who shook his head in anticipation of their questions. Val would not see them. "Not at home to visitors" was how he put it.

"No one is home?" Oscar asked. "Not even Lord and Lady Wharton?"

"Gone as well, and half the household staff with them. Trip to Ireland to visit some cousins."

"How long have they been gone?"

"Left the same day as the child, sir."

Penny gasped. "Gone? She is gone?"

"Sent away to boarding school, miss. Two days after she came here."

"No!"

"Yes, miss. Not the proper place for a youngster, a bachelor's abode."

"Especially a bachelor in his cups," Oscar muttered.

"Quite right, sir."

"You will tell him I leave for Derbyshire in two days' time?" Oscar asked.

Penny felt fresh disappointment at the words.

"I will, sir." The butler nodded.

"And will you tell me the name of the boarding school? That I might write to her?" Penny asked.

Yarrow stood silent a moment, blank-faced, before he said in the mildest of tones, "That information, miss, you must ask of Master Wharton."

"But he refuses to see me."

"Yes, miss. I am very sorry, miss."

They went away, unsatisfied.

"And so, I am to lose your company as well, Mr. Hervey?" Penny said sadly as Oscar saw her home.

He turned to look at her. "Aye. Must return the gray to Cupid."

Cupid. Strange how the name was sufficient to trigger within her a profound state of longing, the image of him springing full to mind.

"Shall I ever have the pleasure of seeing you again?"

He looked surprised she should ask.

"Must come back this way someday," he said. "The fishing is unsurpassed."

"And Mr. Shelbourne?" She felt awkward, asking him—transparent.

He shrugged. "I've no notion as to his plans."

A crow flew across the road ahead of them, cawing hoarsely.

"I pray you find his nephew well," she said.

"I shall inform him of your kind wishes."

"Please do," she said, her hand on his arm, adding urgency to her request. "And thank you."

"I don't know what for," he said. "It's a fishing

expedition we've been on today, and nothing to show for it."

"You are wrong," she protested. "We know more than we did. That is something."

Strong words, no tremor in her voice, and yet she blinked back tears, plunged into a fresh state of despair.

Chapter Eighteen

The fells greened, and the crows were nesting, and every day Penny went to the manor to speak to Val—to gain word of her dear little Felicity.

"Master Valentine is not at home to visitors," Yarrow croaked daily, as dour as any blackbird. She grew to expect as much.

"Will you see to it that he forwards these things to Felicity?" she asked, handing him a box of clothes, puzzles, and books—the fifth such box. "And this doll?" A doll with button eyes and a dress made of the same poplin as one of Felicity's own. "It is very dear to her."

"Yes, miss. Indeed, I will."

"Can you tell me nothing of her, Yarrow? Has not Val seen fit to tell you her direction? Does he pass along my letters?" she asked this morning as she did every morning, sure that eventually he would seek out some word for her if only to stop her asking.

"I regret to say that I have no word from Master Wharton," he said, no regret visible in his austere features.

"And Val?" She changed her pattern this morning in asking. "How does he fare? Is he well with his parents gone? I have not seen him about in the village since his friends' departure."

"Master Valentine . . ." He paused, and the faintest trace of emotion touched his features. So quickly did it pass she could not be sure just what the emotion was. "He has received a letter."

"From Felicity?"

"No. Mr. Shelbourne."

"Oh?"

"Master Valentine speaks of joining his friend."

"Does he?" She felt a twinge of jealousy, that Cupid wrote to Val and not to her, that he wished for Val's company.

"I shall tell him you most kindly asked after his health," Yarrow said as he closed the door.

Heart aching, she mounted Archer, the pony Felicity had loved above all the others, and set off for home, by way of Caesar's Tower, as it was called, though to her mind it would always be Lady Anne's tower. She thought of Cupid, of what he might have said to Val in a letter—of what he might have said to her, had he written.

The fells beckoned, their quiet solitude akin to her own, and thus a comfort to her when melancholy threatened, but she had gone no farther than the old sycamore on the green nearby when she heard hoof-beats and turned to look back.

A man on a bay followed, the flag of pale hair familiar, the wind whipping Val's cloak, a dark cloud against the pale stone backdrop of castle and keep. The bay horse he rode tossed its head, as if the reins bound its mouth too tight.

She turned the pony to meet him.

Val cocked his head, pale hair blown wildly askew, blue smudges beneath his eyes, an air of weariness and dissipation weighing his posture. She wondered if he could possibly be drunk at this hour of the morning and assumed he was. He swayed in the saddle.

"Penny, Penny, Penny," he drawled, his horse towering, a dangerously lascivious gleam lighting his eyes. "You wanted me? You have wanted me every day now for how many weeks?"

She looked about her, at the empty castle, at the windswept vacant road. Her bonnet cut off sight of him briefly. The wind riffled her skirt. When she looked up from batting it down, his gaze lingered on her legs.

"I wanted news of the child," she said bluntly. "Will you forward her things? Better yet, will you give me her direction, that I might send them? Write her?"

"The child, the child, always the child," he grumbled, his handsome nose gone scarlet in the wind. "Do you think of nothing else, my dear?" He guided the bay closer to Archer, calf brushing her knee as he drew alongside. In his gloved hand something glinted. "Do you not remember the night I gave you this?"

Penny frowned. "That is Felicity's locket. Why do you not let her keep it?"

He smiled at that and leaned close to catch a lock of her hair upon gloved hand. "Did you think of me, Penny my love, when I went away to war?"

She pulled away, surprised, the tug on her hair making her scalp tingle unpleasantly. "I did," she admitted.

The bay crowded the pony, so that their legs were trapped, side by side, between the warm bellies of their mounts.

"Do you think of me now?" He leaned close, the smell of whiskey on his breath, the scarf at his throat slapping one ill-shaven cheek.

She recognized desire in his world-weary gaze, and thought of the night he had left her, remembering distantly how charming he had been, how close she had come to falling head over heels. She felt no pull for him now, nothing at all other than pity.

"Have you none of the passion of that night left in you, my dear? Your mother's passion?" His gaze roved over her with far more familiarity than she could stomach.

The pony, as uneasy as she with his proximity,

snorted and made a move to step away. He grabbed at the cheek strap with one hand and dared settle the other upon the pommel around which her legs were bent. The wind, contrary creature, covered his hand with the wayward edge of her skirt.

"My mother . . ." Heat flared in her cheeks while a chill settled in her nether regions. She knew nothing of her mother, other than that she looked like the painting above her father's bed, other than her secret. She considered a moment telling him the truth, but stopped herself—no purpose served other than to salve her ego.

"Does she still warm the bed of some handsome gypsy king?" he drawled in an offensive tone.

"She is dead," she said flatly.

That gave him pause, but not for long. "And you?" he asked. "Has the fire within you gone out, as well? Or is it banked embers I see in your eyes?" His hand strayed, caressing her calf.

She slapped at the arm that had once held her, with her quirt and turned the pony. "I will not make the same mistake again."

He nursed his knuckles, heat again in his eyes, this time of anger as he called out, "A pity."

She halted the pony, turning in the saddle, the wind very cold on her cheek, her ears, nose, and fingertips chilled. "I would remind you of the consequences of your last bout of foolishness."

The bay snorted, as if expressing an opinion.

He shrugged, gloved hands impatient on the reins. "You are like a broken music box, with but one refrain. Have you been loved by no one since I went away? Would you change your tune, I wonder, if I were Cupid bent on sweeping you away?"

"As Eve was?" she bit out.

"Eve?" He stared at her blankly, then laughed. "Oh! Would you call men snakes, then?"

"Snake, indeed. You do not so much as ask what happened to her."

He frowned, confused. "Her?"

The bay raised its tail. The odor of fresh dung engulfed them.

"Eve. Evie Branwaithe."

Still he stared at her without comprehension, the stench all too appropriate.

"Felicity's mother," she said impatiently.

His brows rose. The puzzled look was undiminished. "Eve of Appleby?" He frowned as the bay shook its head and stepped away from its own effluence. "Felicity's mother? But . . . everyone said . . ."

"Everyone said?" She stared at him, astonished. "Of course everyone said. I have led everyone else to believe what they wanted to believe. It was best for Felicity that they think I was her mother rather than the local strumpet. But, Val! You were there. Surely you remember."

He blinked, slow-witted. "I remember sweet kisses, your arms wound about my neck. I remember even sweeter lovemaking, all of you wound about—"

"No." Fire flooded her cheeks. She shook her head, hands so tight on the reins the pony backed a step. "Kisses, yes. I offered them freely. I thought . . . I thought myself in love with you. I thought you cared for me above all others. You said as much. Do you remember?"

He said nothing, his attention turned inward, trying to recall.

"You asked too much," she whispered.

He shook his head. "No."

"You went to her." The now distant pain gave the words an unexpected tremulousness.

"No, no!" He spoke with vehemence, the bay suddenly sidestepping, nervous beneath him. Confusion twisted features she had once considered dear.

"How could you?" she asked. "How could you go straight from the warmth of my arms to her bed?"

His head shook in denial. "I . . . I've no memory of it."

"You had been drinking."

"Drinking?" He laughed, a bitter sound. "I was drunk," he said, as if it were a jest. "I have been drunk these six years and more."

The wind kicked last year's leaves across the road with a hollow rattle. The pony shook its head.

"Perhaps it is time you stopped," she said, the suggestion sensible enough to her way of thinking.

He laughed. Oh, how he laughed. It rang out like a clarion, setting birds to flight, lifting the bay on its hind legs, hooves lashing the air. He kept his seat. "Ha! Just like that? You sound like Cupid. Stupid Cupid. He is forever telling me to stop. Just stop. As if it were an easy thing."

He turned the still jittery bay, chuckling harshly.

"But how much of your life is forgotten?" she called after him. "Lost? Remembered falsely?"

"Don't you understand?" He flung the words over his shoulder, slow and sarcastic, as if explaining to an idiot. "I do not want to remember."

"The war?" she asked of his back, the wind catching her words.

He laughed harshly. "What a ridiculous question. Of course the war."

"But the war is over," she said.

"Ah!" he said snidely, looking back at her, his lip curled. "Thank you so very much for pointing out the blindingly obvious."

She gigged the pony to follow. "What memories were you drowning before the war?" she shouted, angry now.

"What?" Face red with pique, he jerked the bay to a wall-eyed standstill.

"The night before you left, the night you went to Eve. Why were you drunk then?"

He wiped at his mouth, as if to remove a bad taste. He barked a short laugh. "I was afraid."

Afraid?

"That the fighting would be over before my ship sailed. I worried"—his voice seethed with bitterness—"that I should never have another opportunity—that all the fighting might be finished before I had a chance to try my hand. Fool!" he shouted. "Fool!"

Spurring the bay much more roughly than the creature deserved, he rode back the way he had come.

Chapter Nineteen

Alexander sped down the steps of the elegant Georgian country house that he considered home—for the moment. He had been born here, reared here, and yet . . . it was more his elder brother Simon's house than his, Simon's birthright. He had felt the truth of it most strongly upon his return. His sisters were married and gone to live elsewhere. His parents had aged greatly in his absence, and Simon and his wife took up residence as if it were already theirs. The servants answered to their command. Their child had been born here. Lost here. The heir's heir—a loss that was felt keenly by all.

He felt it keenly—in so many ways. As keenly as he felt out of place. No one knew what to say when he told them he had quit the 95th, had shed the feathered shako and all it stood for, for good.

The questions were voiced in their eyes. *What will you do now? Where will you live? How do you mean to make a living if not in the military?* He longed for answers himself. He longed for a sense of place—and thought often of Appleby, of the touch-me-not.

He greeted the approach of the hired coach with lightened heart despite the bleakness of his mood. Arms wide, he met Oscar's descent from the carriage.

"I bring you the gray," Oscar said, stepping to the rear of the wheels, where the poor, dust-coated animal was tied. As they led the creature around the house to the stables, boots crunching on gravel, Oscar gave

Alexander's black armband a squeeze. "I wish my visit might be on happier terms. My condolences."

"Yes," Alexander replied with a heavy sigh. "A promising lad. He will be sorely missed. Most especially by my sister-in-law. She is quite prostrate with grief."

Oscar fingered his mustache. "Are you sure my visit is not ill-timed?"

Alexander smiled. "I have been missing your much abused mustache."

Oscar stopped his fidgeting with a sheepish grin.

"And . . . I . . . have been longing to hear news of . . ."

"Val? He refused visitors, you know? Have not seen hide nor hair of him since the day you left, though I did stand thrice weekly upon his doorstep, and frequented the pub he was said to favor."

Alexander looked him in the eye. "Not Val."

Oscar's eyes widened in surprise. A smile touched his lips. He made a move to stroke his mustache, then stopped himself. "Not Val you are hankering to hear of? Well, I've much to tell you of my luck at fishing. One could not wish for better waters than the Eden."

Alexander could not keep his lips from twitching with amusement. "Fish tales can wait. It is—"

Oscar lifted a hand. "Let me guess. Could it be Miss Foster you would hear news of?"

Alexander nodded. "I have fresh appreciation for what she must be suffering in the loss of a child. You went to her, as I asked?"

Oscar's smile faded. "Indeed I did. And together we called upon Val, with no more luck than when I called upon him alone."

A lad ran out from the stables to take the gray.

"See to it he has water and a well-deserved rubdown." Alexander clapped the horse affectionately on the flank.

The lad touched his cap and led the animal away.

Alexander returned to the house by way of the rose garden, picking up their conversation as if there had been no interruption. "How did she seem?"

Oscar stopped to admire the neatly clipped garden. He bent to finger a thorny branch, rosebuds still tight and green on the bright new growth. "Did you know it really is a flower?"

"What?"

"The touch-me-not? Looks rather like a tiny pansy in purple and yellow. A native to the lakes."

"No. I did not know. Studying the local flora and fauna, Oscar?"

"They were growing by the wayside. We walked right past them. She pointed them out."

"Penny?"

"Yes. Knew their significance, too. Didn't say anything directly to the point, mind you, but she wore this slightly wounded look as she mentioned their name."

"I see," Alexander said, wishing he had been there.

"As to how she is . . ." Oscar drew a deep breath. "She's missing the girl, right enough, and yourself, as well. Asked after you, and your nevvie, and sent you her prayers and best wishes. It did surprise me, though."

"What?"

Oscar scratched at his chin.

"She seemed resigned to the child's new situation, more so than I might have expected. She had, in fact, spoken to Val the day before I left, and seemed glad the lass had been sent away to school. She did not know which one."

Alexander frowned. "What exactly did she say?"

Oscar gazed at the sky a moment, thinking. "She said, 'Best for the child, given Val's sensibilities, and wise of him to realize as much'."

"That's delightfully ambiguous. Did she say anything else?"

"Asked if we were coming back for Fiona's wedding. Said Fiona had asked. I told her I did not think so, given that you might be in mourning."

Alexander frowned. "And her response?"

"Said the strangest thing, she did."

"Oh?"

"Yes. Made me wonder as to her meaning. Said, 'Better to come back for a wedding than to wait for another funeral.' "

"Who's dying? For God's sake, man, is she suicidal?"

"Miss Foster?" Oscar looked shocked. "The idea never crossed my mind."

Penny stood above the abyss, looking down, considering her mother's choice, wondering what it would feel like to step over the edge, no ground beneath her feet, the rocks below rushing up to meet her.

The wind moaned, hollow and pained, tugging at her hair, pushing her back from the edge.

The banns for Fiona's wedding had been read in church the past three Sundays. Nails in her coffin, daggers in her heart, and she must smile as they were driven home. No such announcements figured in her future, no such happy buzz of gossip. What was she to do now with little hope of marriage, even less of children? Was her future consigned to sheep and stone fences and never-ending contempt in the eyes of all who looked upon her without ever knowing what they saw? Would she begin to believe the image of herself reflected there?

She shivered and drew her shawl close. Above her a kestrel keened, wings dark against the sky. Had there been a moment in falling, that her mother felt free as this bird? What final straw had tipped the scales, driven her violent flight? What demons of doubt, fear, and misery had whispered in her ears? Were they worse than the ones plaguing her daughter, as she considered a future, without Felicity, without

Cupid, her reputation misunderstood due to her own deliberate misdirection?

She had asked Cupid for a valentine he could not deliver—to open the world's eyes to who she really was. It was too much to ask of any man. She did not deserve the luxury of disappointment, and yet she was.

Hoofbeats behind her, she turned, stepping away from the ravine, expecting her father once again, completely unprepared for Val. He looked rather the worse for wear astride his lathered bay, his hair tousled, his coat much wrinkled, purple shadows beneath bloodshot eyes.

"Penny, my lucky Penny, always turning up where I least expect to see you. On Wharton land, no less." He cocked his head to one side as he used to do when he was a youth, fair hair falling in troubled eyes, the bay restless beneath him. "You do not mean to jump, do you? I have heard this promitory has been used to such end."

She wondered if he knew how much his words goaded her. But no, he was more likely drunk than malicious.

"Val." She inclined her head. "How does your daughter fare?"

He brushed aside the question as if it were an annoying fly and stilled the horse, his hand stroking its sweated neck. "Do you not care how I fare, sweet Penny?" he asked, sadness in the set of his mouth. "Would you not ask after my health?"

"No need," she said. "I see, plain enough, you are ill."

"Ill and suffering," he agreed. "Half sober, you see. I would try to stop downing the demon drink, as you did recommend. It is a hell I am cast into. Never has my throat felt so parched, my memory so muddled. I ride that I might not reach always for the bottle. But, tell me, Penny. What brings you here, my dear, alone on the deserted fells, not so much as your dog for company?"

"My mother brings me," she admitted.

His eyes gleamed. Bluer than robin's eggs she had once thought them. "A bit of wildness, is it?" he leaned forward in the saddle, leather creaking. "Hunting gypsies, are you, my dear?"

She laughed, which made him sit back, fair brows rising.

"Not gypsies, no. Answers," she said.

"Are they to be found here?" he asked wistfully, his head turning to regard with bleak expression the emptiness of the fells.

She shook her head and wrapped her arms about herself. "My mother may have, but I find only questions, Val."

"What sort of questions?"

She shrugged off her own hands and forced herself to look him directly in the eyes as she walked past the nose of his horse. "I wonder how she could have abandoned me to another's care."

He frowned.

She kept walking, stopping for no more than a moment to fling a question back over her shoulder. "How does your daughter, Val?"

He spurred the bay alongside her just long enough to mutter irritably, "Such a question serves naught, my dear Penny, but to renew my thirst."

He was hard on the horse, she thought, too hard, in spurring the bay away from her.

The post coach and its attendant cloud of dust broke through the trees, rounded the bend, and passed Penny Foster on her pony on the road that skirted the pale medieval castle of Appleby. She did not look up as they bowled by. Her shoulders wore a dejected slump, even the pony's head hung low, the reins held slack, but she was alive, by God, and a vision of loveliness to Alexander. He came very close to throwing himself out of the coach to set off in pursuit.

"Steady, lad." Oscar recognized his intent, stopping him with a touch. "She cannot get far."

And when the coach at last came to a proper halt at the King's Head, Oscar flung open the door and urged, "After her now. I shall see to our bags."

Alexander shared with his friend a brief look of deepest knowing and appreciation before he plunged into the sunshine, setting off toward the castle. Her pony was no longer to be seen on the road, but a pile of fresh dung lured him through the trees, and up the slight rise that led through the gatehouse archway. Before him stretched a green, and ivy-draped wall. To his left loomed the castle, to his right the taller, boxier keep. He might never have found her had the gate-keeper not come down the set of stairs behind him in that instant and politely asked his business.

"A young lady came this way . . ." he began.

"Is it Penny Foster do you mean?"

Alexander nodded.

"Ah, yes." The gatekeeper smiled and rocked on his heels. "Come to see our Great Picture again, dear Penny."

"Great picture?"

"Lady Anne."

"Yes," he said, remembering how she had once muttered that name. "Lady Anne. Where might I find her?"

The old man led the way, coattails flapping, heels ringing briskly on stone, leaving him at the doorway to the echoing Great Hall. She stood at the far end, her back to him, examining a triptych with unwavering concentration. She could not help but hear his approach. His footsteps echoed, and yet she did not turn until he was almost upon her, and then the bonneted head swiveled, and she caught her breath in a gasp.

"You! You have come back!"

*   *   *

She stood stunned, afraid her imagination had run away with her, afraid he would disappear. But no, the grief trapped in his eyes and the black armband on his sleeve were all too real.

Noticing the direction of her gaze, he looked past her to the triptych.

"I am so very sorry for your loss," she said.

He spoke at the same time, as if to drown out her condolences. "Who is this Lady Anne that you visit?"

They fell silent simultaneously before he said very quietly, "I appreciate your concern." Sadness hung uneasily in eyes suddenly bright with moisture.

"Lady Anne once lived here," she said, turning to the triptych, allowing both of them a moment to recover. She pointed to the first panel, an attractive dark-haired girl, stiffly formal in fan collar and fine dress, musical instruments at her feet, books on the wall behind her. "Here she is at fifteen. Her father had just died. He is in the center panel with her mother and two brothers who came before her and died as children."

He studied the figures intently. "She was young to bear such losses."

"Yes," she said. "I have always thought we were kindred spirits."

He cocked his head, regarding her with some of the same sadness she had exhibited for his personal loss. "Your mother left you as an infant, didn't she?"

"She died," she whispered, unable to look at him.

He made no sudden movement or exclamation to evidence his surprise; no, it was his stillness she noticed from the corner of her eye.

"I had heard . . ."

"Gypsies?" She laughed harshly, the noise echoing—too loud. She cut the sound short and dared to look at him. "Poor Gypsies. Too long have they been falsely accused." She sighed, then looked once more at the portrait, nervous fingers pleating the fabric of her skirt. "No. She killed herself."

He opened his mouth, as if to say something.

She stopped him by speaking first. "And so I adopted Lady Anne as surrogate mother. She did great things, our Lady Anne: building almshouses, raising chapels and churches from the ashes of destruction and neglect, extensively renovating five castles, Appleby's among them, and all after she reached the age of sixty."

Killed herself. The words still resounded in the silences between them.

She tapped the third panel. "That was when Lady Anne finally came into the inheritance denied her since her father's death."

She dared another look at him. He appeared to be extremely interested in the familiar portrait of the still attractive if much older Anne, dark hair falling in waves across a full white collar, a pup at her knee, the books at her back in disarray, well thumbed.

She could not keep her eyes from his profile, the dark bristling hair she so longed to touch, the lengthy black lashes that flickered as he turned to look at her.

"She sounds a fine model." His gaze searched hers, as if he would know everything, as if he might read the answers to the questions of a lifetime in her eyes.

"Yes," she agreed, a little shaken, unsure she wanted any man to read her so intently. She drew strength from Lady Anne. "Well read—clever in history and the classics. She outlived two husbands and three children."

"Sounds like a lonely sort of life."

She had no answer for that.

"A woman of stamina." He filled the gap.

"Exactly. A woman who squeezed all that she could out of the troubled life that was given her."

Unlike her mother in every way, she thought.

It would seem he read her mind.

"Your mother . . ."

She regarded the scuffed toes of her shoes. "I know virtually nothing of her, other than that she suffered from melancholy, and did not care to hear me cry."

His turn for silence. The words hung between them, seemingly brutal and uncaring.

"Your father . . ." he said at last.

She sighed, and went to one of the tall windows and stared out over the bowling green. "He does not speak of her. And I do not ask."

He followed her. Quiet and gentle, his approach, the light from the window full on his face, no hiding his sympathy. He smelled of bay leaf and the road dust powdering his hat and hair, and she could see in that moment what he would look like as an older man. She wondered if she would still have the privilege of knowing him then.

"Had you special need of Lady Anne today?" he asked.

"Yes." She licked her lips, then stepped away from the painting and tucked her hand into the crook of his elbow, both comforted and aroused by such physical contact. "I was missing Felicity today, more than usual. And . . . and . . ."

He gave her hand a gloved pat, and still she felt the tingle of his touch. "What? You can tell me anything, you know. I am your Cupid."

She bit down upon her lips before blurting, "Why did you return?"

"The wedding," he said.

She stared at him blankly a moment, lips parted, hope rising, before it all fell into place, deflating her. "Oh! Of course, Fiona's wedding."

Chapter Twenty

The day of Fiona's wedding dawned clear and bright, perfect weather for a happy union, perfect cloudless skies for the outdoor celebration that would follow the ceremony. Penny stepped into the dim, echoing confines of St. Lawrence's, smile at the ready, with every expectation that the next three days were going to be difficult, if not unbearable. She was glad for Fiona, of course. One could not look upon a smile that beamed so brightly without some gladness, and yet, the moment she looked away, sadness possessed her heart. How removed she felt from these proceedings, how distant. As Eve must have felt, so long ago. Poor Eve.

Sight of Alexander and Oscar in the pews ahead of hers lifted her spirts momentarily, but here was sadness and a coming parting of the ways, too. They would be gone with the end of the festivities.

She took no comfort as the ceremony began, in thinking her life might be like Lady Anne's—that she might not come into her best and most productive years until she was sixty. She could not bear the thought of it. And so, she set her chin most firmly and resolved to enjoy herself, even if joy was to be found only in staring at the back of Cupid's head.

A wave of whispering turned Alexander's head. He looked right at her, eyes widening with pleasure, a smile dawning, the expression fleeting as he looked past. A frown took its place.

She must turn to see what clouded his brow.

Val had arrived. A rather untidy Val, chin ill-shaven, neck cloth sagging. His hair looked as if it had not seen a proper combing in days. He was dressed for a wedding, well enough, but his once proud military bearing was gone, his handsome face transformed—cheeks hollow, eyes bloodshot, the skin beneath them like blue parchment. Only when he smiled was there some semblance of the old Val to be seen, and he was not wont to smile so much as he once had. He walked rather unevenly down the aisle to the family pew, his progress stopping even the vicar, mid word, so that the groom turned, and finally, her eyes very round, the bride.

Val waved a nonchalant hand, his words faintly slurred. "I do beg your pardon. Had every intention of arriving promptly. Overslept, you see. Do go on."

The vicar did just that, but the congregation took some time in settling. More than one whispered hiss marred the reading of the vows. Penny's own thoughts were distracted by the litany of doubt that ran over and over in her mind. It was to this man Felicity looked for guardianship. It was on him her future depended.

As if he read her thoughts, Alexander turned briefly to look her way, concern marking his features, concern in his dark green eyes. She had to admit to herself in that moment that she found comfort in his gaze, as she had from the moment they had first met on the road into Appleby.

She looked drawn, he thought, tired and worried—stark contrast to the merry faces gathered to witness this wedding—not quite so changed as Val, by heavens, but their time apart had weighed a heavy hand upon the light in her eyes. He would change that if it were within his power.

He thought of his Valentine promise to her as the

vows were read, imagining how he might open the world's eyes to view her as he saw her, this Penny of unknown value, this gallant young woman, unlike any he had ever met. Who among those gathered here knew, as he did, that she took comfort, had found strength and mothering in a painted history of a woman long dead? Who among them realized she had thrown away her own good name that a child might not be despised as the daughter of the local whore? Had she revealed to no one else the dark secret of her mother's end? The gypsy lie that cast ill shadow upon her own nature? Did anyone but he know how much she sacrificed of self, for her father, for her mother, and for Felicity?

How much of oneself could a person give away, he wondered, before there was nothing left?

He imagined himself standing, declaring these truths before the entire congregation. He imagined leading her to the front of the church, that all might see her with fresh eyes. Would the truth be believed? In looking about, at the faces of those gathered, he doubted it.

And if truth could not change the world's view of her in this place of saints and angels, what might? How did one go about opening eyes to truths people did not want to see?

In the couple before him stood the answer. *Marriage.* Did not marriage above all else make a real difference in the way a woman was regarded? He almost laughed out loud. *Of course!* He must marry her.

A frightening thought, and yet it was at the same time exhilarating. Why had he not realized as much before? He must marry her.

Would she have him? he pondered. Did she sense the truth of his feelings for her? His growing respect and affection? Indeed, his love for her? Would she have him if he asked? He had so little to offer—no prospect of wealth, no fixed career. He had, in fact, little idea what he should do with his future other than to stop killing people.

Before him, the wedding band was placed upon the beaming bride's plump finger. Fiona Gilpin, now Fiona Greenlow, looked beautiful in her happiness, transformed. Alexander smiled. He vowed in that moment to bring just such a sparkle to a pair of amethyst eyes one day.

No sooner had the thought crossed his mind than a shout went up and a half dozen young men bolted from their pews and raced for the doors. Laughing, the congregation stood and followed them a little more circumspectly, the newlyweds among them.

Alexander made a point of falling in beside Miss Foster, leaving Oscar to his own devices. When she turned her head to look up at him, he smiled and asked, "Why the big hurry?"

"Brandy," she said, smiling back at him, mischief in her eyes. When he met her answer with confusion, she explained, "A footrace to the bride's house. Winner to return here with two bottles of brandy, meant to toast the newlyweds. I believe a new pair of shoes was named as prize. There are several races scheduled to be run, on foot and on horseback. Wrestling, as well. Do you care to compete?"

Was there a hint of a challenge in her question?

Val answered for him. He leaned heavily over their shoulders, smelling of spirits. "Oh, but Penny, my pet, it is the shooting competition he must apply himself to, if only to show Cumberland why he is called Cupid."

Alexander met him with a smile, but shook his head. "I shall leave the honors to you and Oscar, old friend."

"What?" Val barked in disbelief.

Alexander shrugged. "I've no desire to pick up firearms of any kind, ever again."

"Gone soft, have you?"

"If it is soft to be quit of killing things, then yes."

Val laughed too loud. "Even to the killing of paper targets?"

Alexander held his peace, his eyes on Penny, and hers on him—and in the jewel of her gaze he thought he saw a hint of admiration, even understanding.

No such emotion touched Val's puzzled look. "As you will." He stepped past them, saying wryly, "I shall doubtless carry away the prize if you would leave it to me. Oscar has not so sharp an eye for targets."

His hand is steadier, Alexander could not help thinking as Val walked away. He turned to find Penny looking at him quizzically.

"Why are you called Cupid?"

When he did not immediately respond, she said, "I assumed it had something to do with your being a friend of Val's and equally talented in charming the ladies, but I am mistaken, am I not?'

"You do not find me charming?"

"Such a simple question and yet you avoid answering. It has something to do with your shooting, hasn't it?"

He said nothing.

She cocked her head with a quiet little smile and kept looking at him, as if she saw right through him. Not even the runners who came charging back into the churchyard at that point, bearing the bottles of brandy, to the tune of much shouting and loud cheers, could divert her focus.

Glasses were handed round, courtesy of the local pub from whence the brandy had been purchased, and rousing toasts made, the entire party invited at that point to accompany the bride and groom to their new home, where the festivities were to continue.

"May I offer you . . ." Alexander turned, his arm out, only to find Penny gone. She had stepped back inside the cool dark of the church. He could see the pale flash of her skirt. Following, he found her standing before one of the tombs, hand outstretched, angels looking down on her.

"Penny?"

She raised her head, stepping back, hand falling.

He need not ask whose resting place this was. The name had been cast in stone—Lady Anne Clifford, born: Jan 30, 1590—died: March 26, 1676 and beside her, Margaret Russell Clifford, her effigy in alabaster.

"Lady Anne and her mother," Penny said softly, as if afraid to disturb the dead. "They were as close in life as they are in death."

The tombs were hip to hip. "They must have been close, indeed," he said.

Her eyes gleamed in regarding the headstones. The set of her jaw went soft. "On the road to Penrith there stands a pillar emblazoned with Lady Anne's coat of arms. It marks the spot where these two last bade each other farewell."

"Sweet testament," he said.

She nodded. "At a dole stone nearby, Lady Anne annually distributed alms to the poor, in memory of her mother."

"How kind," he said, beginning to think her unwholesomely obsessed with the Lady Anne.

She looked up at him, face pale and perfect in the darkness, her mouth enticing. "Are you close to your mother?" The question echoed wistfully, quenching all lustful thoughts.

"Yes." He indicated the tombs. "Not this close, but I think you would like her. She is as fond of dogs as you are."

His words stilled her a moment, and a trace of pleased surprise touched her features. "Is she?"

"Yes. I hope to introduce you someday."

"I would like that."

How serious she looked.

He held out his arm.

She took it.

He drew her close. "I am called Cupid because I always shot for the heart," he admitted. "My battalion found it odd."

She did not pull away, as he had anticipated. To the contrary, she leaned closer, her eyes liquid with concern. A long moment of silence ensued there in the gloomy echoing quiet as her gaze searched his, asking without ever voicing the question, *Why?*

"I would not have them suffer," he said, with every hope she would not despise him for what he had done.

"Of course," she whispered giving his arm a squeeze. "Of course." And in the echoing sibilance of her reply, he thought he heard the voices of angels.

Penny knew that her every move was followed by whispers, by gossip, by speculation.

That the Fosters took up both Mr. Shelbourne and his friend Oscar, while Val rattled along in an otherwise empty carriage, was noted and remarked upon by the citizens of Appleby, as was the perception that Val and his friend Cupid seemed a trifle distant. That Val had arrived late, unkempt and quite likely drunk, could not avoid mention either. It was assumed by many that these three things were in some way connected. Speculation ran rampant as the wedding party set off across the Eden by way of the ancient bridge that led into the Sands. They went on foot, on horseback, and by carriage, beribboned Morris dancers leading, a tin pipe making the way merry, laughter ringing on a balmy breeze.

Past Shire Hall and the bowling green they proceeded to the newlyweds' cottage. Gossip kept pace. The carriage was full with Oscar and Cupid on one side, facing Penny and her father on the other, knees bumping, eyes meeting with warmth—with understanding. Cupid's eyes held a growing affection—undeniable affection. He cared for her. The real question was, how much?

Fiona's new husband had housed himself for several years in the little stone cottage before which everyone gathered. A grove of budding apple trees stretched to the rear of the house, a vegetable garden to one side, stables on the other. All were dwarfed in this instant by the crowds of people, carriages, and horses that engulfed the spot.

Fiona's pink-cheeked husband was carrying a blushing Fiona across the threshold as they arrived, and no sooner had the majority of the witnesses shouted their approval than they came out again, followed by four lads who bore the bride's cake from the cottage on a raised platform, ribbons whipping in the wind.

A brown crown, the cake was raised above Fiona's garlanded head, and amid much laughter and inevitable blushes, it was broken above her, the first piece tasted by bride and groom, who declared it the best bride's cake ever.

The bride's blushes deepened as a garter was removed from one plump, white-stockinged leg, to be wildly flung among the local bachelors, who jumped high in a struggle over the catching of it.

As the troupe of fiddlers started up music for dancing, and bottles of sack, claret, and wine were liberally poured, Penny and Alexander took their cake and libation between two rows of the apple trees. Finding a stump to sit upon, they sat to enjoy the buttery, almond-flavored confection.

Above them the tree branches made music in the wind. Before them, the bride's father led his daughter in the first dance on the greening sward of winter-dried grasses already much trampled by the guests' carriages. A pretty sight, to see the old man so gallant. It garnered cheers. The two were soon joined by a host of lively dancers.

Penny watched them, cake forgotten.

"Do you dream of such a wedding?" Alexander asked.

She could not go on thinking of him as Cupid now that she knew the truth.

Penny picked at the cake, licking crumbs from her fingertips. "Small chance of that."

He tapped at the corner of his mouth. She licked her lower lip, sure he pointed out crumbs.

"Why so?"

He still stared at her mouth. She dabbed at the corner with her napkin. "There are men hereabouts who would have me," she said, "but not to wife."

He leaned forward, his eyes still fixed on her lips, and brushed the ball of his thumb against the corner of her mouth, pity in his gaze.

She flinched away from so forward a touch, cheeks flushing to think he might believe her ruined, as everyone else did—that he believed her pitiable.

Ducking her head, she said softly, "I am not, you know."

He begged no explanation, simply raised her chin with the crook of his finger, his gaze very warm. The look in his eyes brought tears to hers.

"Do you remember what you asked of me on Valentine's Day?"

He leaned closer, his eyes never leaving hers. He meant to kiss her. She could see it was so. And she meant to let him.

"I remember," she whispered, and closed her eyes as he neared.

His breath seared her lips, the caress of his mouth, damply quenching the fire. And she gave herself up to the buttery, almond sweetness of him.

"What have we here?" her father asked.

Penny jumped up, heart racing, cheeks hot, the plate in her lap falling, shattering on a tree root. Her father stood scowling, arms akimbo, between the apple trees.

"I thought I could trust you," he said flatly, the remark directed at Alexander Shelbourne.

Penny took it to heart. He meant her as well.

"You can," she said.

Her father ignored her. "My Penny is not to be trifled with, you know," he said belligerently. "I thought you understood."

"Such was never my intention, sir."

Her father did not want to listen. "Come, my dear." He held out his hand.

She was not one to disobey. Her eyes met Alexander's.

"Sir!" he protested.

Her father waved her ahead of him. "My dear," he said firmly.

Alexander fell into step at her father's heels. "Sir, I beg you wait. Please, I must explain."

"No explanations necessary." His grip on her hand tightened as she pushed her way through the merrymakers, their hurried progress and his grim expression winning them attention on all sides.

"Father!" She tried to slow him. "It's not what you—"

"Hmph!" His grunt silenced her. "I know all too well what young men want of you, Penny."

Heads turned.

Behind them whispers followed, and the thump of Mr. Shelbourne's heels.

"Mr. Foster!" he cried. "Please, sir."

Her father's frown deepened. His steps did not slow.

"Please, Mr. Foster. I would pay court to your daughter. Will you not allow it?" The loud words stilled the whispers, stopping the nearby dancers. Her father came to an abrupt halt, jaw askew.

Penny snapped her mouth shut.

The crowd parted, waiting.

Her father seemed completely at a loss for words.

Cupid knew everyone listened. She read his awareness in the depths of his eyes, as if he expected her to understand—even to support his stance.

"I would consider myself most fortunate, sir, if you

would allow me to openly court your daughter." He made no effort to lower his voice, that all might hear, that those gathered might see her in a new light.

In that moment the pieces fell into place. Here it was—her Valentine request fulfilled.

Her father stammered a response, in favor of Mr. Shelbourne's gentlemanly request. "If Penny is amenable to the idea, of course."

She smiled, though she would rather weep, and gave the slightest of nods, her heart aching, shot through by the keenest of arrows. He would not see her suffer, she thought. He would not see her suffer.

Chapter Twenty-one

The second day of the wedding celebrations dawned fair and still. It seemed a day that held its breath, as motionless as the village when Alexander set out to fetch Penny in a hired gig. As he directed the horse away from the King's Head, he caught sight of a familiar figure walking toward him from the direction of St. Lawrence's, and waved.

The vicar waved back, rather frantically, and called out to him, "Have you a moment, Mr. Shelbourne?"

Alexander stopped the horse and asked him with a smile, "Do you mean to participate in the wedding races today, vicar?"

The vicar shook his head. "No, no. I leave that to younger limbs, lad, and sharper eyes. It is on another matter entirely I would speak with you."

"Where is it you are headed, sir? I would be happy to deliver you."

"Thank you kindly, lad. It is just a wee piece. I wish to call on the widow Brumley."

He climbed promptly into the gig, and when he had settled himself, Alexander said, "Is it Val's drinking brings that worried look to your brow? I must admit it troubles me, and yet I've no idea what I might say or do to dissuade him from imbibing."

The vicar frowned and shook his head, his gaze no less troubled. "Not Val, lad. 'Tis you I've concern for."

Alexander turned to him, surprised. "Me? Whatever for?"

"I do hate to speak ill of any of my parishioners," the vicar said, "but I fear there is much you do not know of the young lady who has chanced to catch your eye."

"Miss Foster?"

"Aye. Poor Penny Foster."

Alexander arrived a quarter of an hour later than expected, and Penny, who could not believe her fortune had changed, began to think he had second thoughts, that he regretted his outspoken commitments of yesterday. Thus it was with wildly beating heart she heard the sound of hoofbeats, and the rattle of carriage wheels on cobblestone in the courtyard.

"I do beg your pardon for my tardiness," he said when she met him at the door.

"It is very kind of you to do this," she said. "But you need not, you know."

"I was waylaid by the vicar." Then his brow wrinkled as her words sank in. "Need not what?"

"You have fulfilled your Valentine promise. You need not continue the charade."

Alexander looked at her most quizzically as he helped her into the hired gig. "Do you not care for my company, Penny?" he asked, looking up at her.

She could feel the heat build in her cheeks. "No, no," she exclaimed.

"I am hurt," he said.

"I mean . . ." She clung to his hand when he would have stepped away. "No, it is not that I do not care for you. I do."

"Do you?"

Abruptly, she released her hold on him, unable to look him in the eyes.

"Of course. You have been very kind."

He stared at her a moment, trying to read the expression she hid beneath the brim of her bonnet, then smiled before rounding the back of the gig and stepping up to settle himself in the narrow seat beside her. His hip rubbed hers, then his shoulder as he picked up the reins. He had no choice, of course; the bench was short.

He tilted his head to look her way, mischief in his eyes. "Do you think I do not truly care for your company?"

"That I cannot speak to."

He laughed and called to the horse, "Walk on."

Then he tipped his head her way again, and eyebrows raised, said, "Can you not?"

"It is just . . ."

"Do you really think I am drawn to you for no more reason than the fulfillment of a Valentine promise?" His hands were firm in guiding the horse, his gloved fingers long and elegant.

"No, but it might be better for you if you were."

"What?"

She stared out at the familiar countryside, eyes glazed, heartsick. "You are the son of a gentleman, of good character and better connections. I am the daughter of mischance and ill assumption. Will not your mother, your father, wish more for you?"

"They would wish me happy."

Such a dear face he had, she mused, such a dear, dear face, to look upon her with such genuine confusion. And she, who loved him, wanted only what was best for him. "But . . ."

He slowed the horse. "Would you warn me away after the vicar himself has failed?"

"The vicar?"

"Yes. Poor man feared I knew not the whole story of your past."

"Oh?"

He smiled as he flicked the reins. The gig leapt forward, the horse at a trot. "Turned out he was the one misinformed."

"Was he?"

"Indeed. Told him as much."

"Did you?" She twisted the edge of her shawl in nervous fingers. "Exactly what did you tell him?"

His eyes twinkled with mirth. "Why, that he ought to have a chat with the barber of Dunston, for if anyone knows the truth of the matter, it is he."

She sat there a moment, staring at the world flashing by—a familiar blur of grass and trees, and yet today they seemed new—changed. "You knew? All this time, you knew, and never told me?"

He chirruped to the horse, his attention on the road that rushed toward them. "I knew from the moment I first saw you." He turned his head, to gaze at her with unguarded affection. "On the road into Appleby."

On this, the second day of the wedding celebrations, the wedding guests gathered again outside the newlyweds' cottage, horses and carriages flattening the grass. Excitement was high. A saddle was to be run for, two bridles to be trotted for, two belts to be wrestled for, two hats to be boxed for, gloves to be leapt for, and three pewter tankards to be shot for.

Penny, who felt she had won the greatest prize of all in Alexander Shelbourne's willing presence at her side, felt no urge to join the footraces, even though wings had been lent to her feet. However, when the three-legged race was announced, Alexander turned to her with a mischievous gleam in his eyes.

"Care to give it a go?"

There lurked an element of danger in such a request. It was generally married men and women who ran the three-legged race. For an unattached female of good reputation to do so invited censure.

And yet, there seemed something both titillating

and entirely appropriate in the idea of binding her leg to his, that they must walk in tandem, as they had in coming down from Nichol's chair.

"Yes," she said, knowing they would create a minor sensation, knowing she ought to say no. Of course, she could not, after all, lay claim to a spotless reputation, and everyone knew it. What further harm could such an entertaining pastime do her?

Looking well pleased with himself, Alexander went away to put their name in the running, returning with a handful of black ribbon.

"Are you ready?" he asked, waving them, and though she said she was, it was a lie. Word was fast in getting about that she meant to participate, and there were men, both young and old, who drew nearer, that they might get a glimpse of her preparation. Nothing sufficiently prepared her either, for the effect her Cupid had on her whenever he drew near— near enough this time to align his shoe with hers, the edges of their soles bumping as he knelt to bind their ankles.

He stood, and she must grab at his coattail or fall over, so natural was her inclination to step away that she almost felled them both.

"Steady." He chuckled low in his throat and braced her position with his arm about her waist, a move that had the men who watched elbowing one another while whispered opinions flew among the women who observed as keenly as did their husbands.

"Yes," she said, feeling a trifle breathless, feeling in this moment as wildly wanton as so many had long assumed her to be. And yet, not entirely so—she adjusted her foot so their ankles did not bang into each other.

"And now," he said, "you must forgive me for taking liberties, but I think we will do better if you remove this." His hand rose to the ribbons beneath her chin, and with a swift tug he had it loosed and lifted

her bonnet away from her head. The breeze fingered
her curls, and she began to feel he undressed her with
far too practiced a hand as he set the hat aside and
bent to lift her skirt. Paying no attention to her gasp
or the raised brows and suggestive grins of the oglers,
he grazed her leg with a gloved hand, then with the
movement of hem and petticoat exposed black stockings to just below the knee.

"You will hold this while I tie?" he asked.

She could not look at those who watched, could not
look at anyone but him, at the spot on the nape of his
neck where his dark bristling hair formed a perfect V.

Wordlessly, she clutched at the hem of her skirt,
swaying against him, clutching at him a little in fact,
though it was her inclination to put some space between them as cold air and warm hands swept beneath
her skirt.

"That's good," he said, looking up with a wink, his
eyes sparkling, as if he enjoyed the moment.

How hot her cheeks felt. How stirring his gloved
hand as he slid another length of black ribbon into
the sensitive hollow at the back of her knee, his hands
touching, fingering, pushing aside petticoat and drooping hem.

"You understand the necessity of my forwardness,"
he said, glancing sideways at her.

"I begin to wonder if this is a good idea," she said,
inhaling sharply as, rising, he pressed the entire length
of his leg most familiarly to hers and tied it snug just
below the knee, the connection of muscled calf moving
against muscled calf wildly stimulating.

Their shoulders bumped when he straightened, all
of him too close, and yet not close enough, their position dizzying, both of them striving for balance. She
was troubled by conflicting desires—either she must
step further away, or closer still. He leaned into her,
saying, "Steady now. We mustn't fall down at the out-
set. Perhaps this will help."

Adjusting his stance, arm sliding about her waist, fitting her shoulder into the hollow of his, he said, "That's better. Can you be comfortable?"

Could she? Comfortable was not at all the word she would have chosen to describe their current posture. How could one be comfortable when every iota of one's being cried out with awareness, with heightened sensitivity to the brush of sleeve to sleeve, and stockinged leg to stockinged leg? Could she be comfortable without him?

He gave her waist a warm squeeze, "You must relax into it for this to work well. Like dancing," he said.

"Like dancing," she echoed.

She focused her attention on relaxing, tensed muscles softening, so that her thigh seemed to mold itself to his, and hip bumped hip. She could feel the ebb and flow of his breathing, by way of his rib cage as it settled against hers.

"Can you feel it?" he asked.

"It?" she repeated, captivated by the laughter in his eyes.

"The difference?" he said, shifting his weight.

She had no choice but to shift with him.

"And now we must try walking." He laughed. "You first."

They were awkward, but soon fell into stride. Penny even allowed herself to enjoy the odd sensation of their combined rolling gait until she looked up with a laugh and found Val watching them with a dour expression.

So forbidding was his regard, she trod unevenly and almost tripped, but Alexander braced her waist and cried, "Watch out!" and with a quick look down at their feet she better focused both mind and body.

When she looked up again, Val was gone, and so fast had the moment passed that she wondered if she had imagined the resentful disenchantment of his features.

*   *   *

They set off at a walk, gaining speed, establishing a common, hip-jolting rhythm, moving in mirrored tandem at a slow run, thigh against thigh, his arm at home about her waist. Alexander could not help but think of other ways in which they two might thump and bump along together as breathless laughter bubbled from their throats and the gathered crowd cheered them on.

They were not the fastest. They could not compete for speed with two long-legged brothers who passed them with gleeful shouts of "Make way. Make way."

But nearing the finish line one brother tripped. With twin oaths the two tumbled. Laughing, Alexander and Penny stumped breathlessly past them, to carry away the prize—matching crystal champagne glasses with which they were urged to toast their success; indeed, their coupled state was commented upon with growing favor. Oscar told them as much as he poured a victory libation.

"And now, you three-legged fool," Val boisterously interrupted as they stood sipping. "Do you mean to join us in the shooting match?" He waved the carbine he held too negligibly at the hunting cronies who followed him like a Greek chorus. "So that you might have a larger vessel for the downing?"

The vessel he referred to was the pewter tankard that stood as prize for the shooting match.

"I leave the prize to you," Alexander said, downing the last of his champagne and handing the glass to Oscar. "Hold that, will you?"

One of the well-muscled lads asked in amazement, "You do not mean to compete?"

Alexander leaned down to untie the ribbons that bound him to Penny, another chance to acquaint himself intimately with the enticing sight of black stockings amidst a froth of white petticoat, a leg he would like to know even better. Blood rushed to his head.

"Cannot be as good as he claims." The tallest lad addressed his fellows.

Alexander paid them no mind, his attention on the loosing of the knot, on the delectable twitch of flesh beneath thin stocking.

The third lad was saying, "Made it all up then, did you? Ha! I'll wager no one's that good."

Oscar leapt to his defense. "You'd lose, lad."

Val's laugh rang flat and humorless.

The black ribbon fell away, loosing their knees. He almost wished he might have left it there, for her leg moved in its freedom, away from his. Her skirts smelled of lavender, and something else, something intriguing and subtle.

He glanced up, feeling flushed—heated. Wanting to leave this argument. Wanting her. She looked not at him, but at Val—a disappointment.

He glanced at Val himself, surprised to find a sad little smile on his lips, a knowing smile, as if Val read his mind.

"Would you not prove yourself, Cupid? Display your prowess?"

Alexander looked down at their shoes, side by side. There were still ankles to untie. "I told you, Val. I've lost all taste for shooting." A hand braced against her hip, he dropped to one knee.

Val loomed over him, swaying. "Oh, but you must, old friend. Prove me an honest man. I have boasted that there is no steadier hand, no keener eye."

This knot was smaller, tighter, the ribbon crushed. It would not easily come undone. Her skirts brushed the side of his head, petticoats rustling. He did not look up. "Kind of you to say so, Val, but I've no intention of competing."

"Lacks courage," someone murmured.

He set his teeth, struggling with it. The ribbon seemed to slide a little. Did he imagine it?

"What do you know of courage, lad?" Val snapped. "I did not see you in uniform, now, did I?"

Alexander closed his eyes and wondered if he ought to cut the ribbon.

"Through the heart, every time, our Cupid," Val persisted. "Never missed a shot."

"Except this one," Alexander said firmly, agitated. Still the knot would not budge.

Her hand brushed his hair. He glanced up into eyes that understood.

"Let it go, Val," Oscar murmured.

"Enough of this," one of the lads said. "We must sign in if we mean to win that tankard."

Their voices grew distant.

The knot gave, slid free, allowing their separation when he would have liked their union better.

She did not move at once, though she must have felt the ribbon fall. She stood, looking down into his eyes, while his hand slid from the back of her knee to the fullness of smoothly stockinged calf. "There," he said.

She stepped aside, and as she moved, skirts wafting lavender, he identified the subtle, musky smell. She wanted him.

"I did not think you serious, Cupid," Val said, unexpected in his return.

Alexander rose, clutching the black ribbons, his eyes for her, and her alone. "I am serious," he said. "Quite serious."

She met his gaze but briefly, lashes falling to hide the desire in her eyes, cheeks flushed.

"Fine words," Val drawled, circling the pair of them. "Noble words. We have, all of us, on occasion, noble intentions, but given the right prize, I daresay even you would change your tune."

Alexander gave him a cursory glance as he wound the black ribbons about the palm of his hand, smoothing wrinkles, wishing Val would join his hunting cronies. "You've nothing to offer that would so tempt me."

"No?" Val watched him wind the ribbons, then cast a suggestive look Penny's way. "Do not be so sure, my friend. I have the notion that you would quite happily join our competition . . ."

"Never."

"Not even if I were to offer, say for instance, the return of a certain young person . . ."

Penny went very still.

"From boarding school."

How pale her face. How solemn the expression with which she regarded Val.

"For what purpose, this return?" Alexander asked.

Val shrugged. "Oh, let us say, to escape an outbreak of the smallpox."

A gasp from Penny. She turned, fear in her eyes.

Val was not yet done. "Said child would, of course, need to be placed in the care of some local woman, someone trustworthy, someone of unblemished reputation."

Alexander frowned.

Val thrust forward the carbine, his hand shaking in the holding of it, and yet he wore the confident look of a conqueror. "Change your mind?"

Alexander could not look at Penny. He knew what she wanted. Instead, he stared at the carbine, forbidden fruit in this Eden, and Val the snake.

"No," he said, then heard the sudden, startled intake of her breath, and still he could not look at her, even when she turned and fled.

He asked flatly, "What is this game, Val?"

"Game?" his onetime friend repeated sarcastically, mouth twisting. "Why, hearts, of course. At what else would Valentine and his Cupid play?"

He came after her, of course, to try to explain, and she did not want to hear, could not imagine anything he might say that would soothe the hurt of his refusal. The ghost of his touch still clung to her knee, her ankle, and she did not know what to do with her feeling for him, did not know what she should say, or think, or feel. She did not want to care again for the wrong man—to find her judgment terribly flawed.

Why would he refuse to help Felicity? It made no sense to her.

"Penny!" he called, and she ignored him, continuing to stride away, the apple trees reaching gnarled arms above her head—tortured-looking trees to bear such wondrous bounty.

"Penny, please!" he called again, this time running. She could hear the thump of his boots, the shortness of his breath.

Lady Anne, Lady Anne, she thought, and leaned into the gnarled trunk of one of the older trees, and waited for him to catch up to her.

"How could you?" She whirled on him as he drew close.

He stopped, several strides distant, his face evidencing concern, and yet he was suddenly a stranger to her.

"You know how much she means to me!" she cried.

He nodded, sadness in his eyes. "Yes."

"As much as a daughter."

"Perhaps too much," he said.

She felt as if he had slapped her. Her thoughts seemed torn from her throat. "Have you never loved anyone so much?"

His lips parted, but no words came.

"A sibling? Your nephew?"

He closed his eyes, then opened them again filled with sadness and something else. Was it pity? For her? It made her angry.

"Yes." The word was no more than a whisper.

Her voice rose. "And yet you would risk her life? The life of a child? I do not understand."

"No." Again the sadness.

"How can you say no to such a simple thing?"

"Not simple at all."

She stared at him, baffled.

"You would ask me to surrender my very soul," he said, his voice low as he bent to pick up a bit of dead branch, and on it a withered apple.

He shocked her to silence.

"On my soul . . ." He cradled the apple a moment, thinking, then held the branch as if it were a carbine, sighting along its length. "I made a sacred vow that I would never take up arms again." The apple dropped to the ground with a dull thud. "Never take another life." He cast aside the stick.

"What about saving a life?"

"The child's?" He toed the fallen fruit and shook his head. "Val would never risk his own daughter. He has sunk low, but not that low."

She stood gazing at him, unconvinced, still fearing for Felicity's safety. "You would not do it for me?"

He sighed, then turned away and shook his head.

Tears burned in her eyes. She pressed her hand to her mouth to stop them, to stop more words, hurtful words, from tumbling free. *Oh, Lady Anne. What can I say to convince him?*

"You must realize that I care for you, Penny," he said, staring up into the trees. "But do not ask me to forsake such a sacred promise. Not even for love's sake."

Love's sake?

And then all joy was taken away from the idea that he loved her in his saying, "I am not given to self-sacrifice, as you are."

Like blows the words hit her. *I am not given to self-sacrifice, as you are.*

It pained her so much that he should say such a thing that she set off again, wanting nothing more at the moment than to be gone from his company, from the potential of more hurtful words. But then it came to her, the perfect question. She could not let it go unasked. Breath catching on a sob, tears streaming unheeded down her cheeks, she turned to him and said, "Do you really think God gave you an extraordinary talent for no better reason than the killing of Frenchmen?"

He looked at her, frowning. "You assume my talent is God-given. What if you are wrong?"

She had no reply for such a question, and so she merely turned her back on him, on the promise of happiness she had once read in his eyes, and weeping, heartbroken, ran away.

Chapter Twenty-two

He was right, of course.

Oscar won the shooting match. Val's aim was off. Master Wharton threw down his gun with an oath, and later had to be carried home, so drunk did he get.

And Penny went home, heart aching, feeling betrayed by the man she had come to trust above all others, turning Alexander Shelbourne's condemnation over and over again in her mind. *I am not given to self-sacrifice, as you are.*

He said it as if self-sacrifice were a bad thing. *Was it?* Was it not worse to be selfish, as he had proven, in refusing to shoot at a target for the sake of a child's safety?

For two days, whatever she was doing, she thought of him with rancor, with pained regret and yearning. On the third day her anger vanished. She was left with nothing but pain and yearning. She wondered when they two might meet again, and mend fences.

He set out on foot that morning from the King's Head under a clouded sky, bird song like laughter on the air. The Eden chuckled beneath the old bridge. The air smelled of fresh-turned earth, of new beginnings, and Alexander was ready to begin again, to put regret and guilt and unfulfilled longing behind him. Where he would go, he was not certain, but he had booked passage out of the valley with the coming week. Today, a nice long walk would clear his head and make him forget his awful parting with Penny Foster, and with Val. If not peace, he might at the very least, gain fresh perspective.

His mind turned in one direction, and his feet in another. Striding over a rise before noon, he was met by the bark of a dog, a flash of black-and-white streaking toward him. The man-eater came not to eat him, but to thrust her head under his hand for a nosing. Then, ears pricked, she raced away again toward the road.

Before him stretched the Foster holdings. The farm had a tidy, prosperous look. The house stood squarely in the middle of the outbuildings, clad in the local, rust-colored sandstone, with slate for a roof. It was not built for a view from its windows, but rather, huddled in the most sheltered spot on the hillside, protected from the winter winds. The barn was of stone, two storied, thick walled, built into the hillside as he approached. The garden patch, rich and dark, contrasted starkly against the white stone wall of the lambing barn, where sheep milled, and the familiar figure of a woman wended her way among them.

With a wry chuckle and new purpose, he set off toward the house. He must speak to her, must try to set things right, or if not right, at least he would bid this woman he had thought to love for the rest of his life, farewell.

The dog, ever alert, was barking again, this time at a man on a horse—a familiar, battle-hardened bay that trotted past the bitch without a sideways glance.

What was Val doing here?

The bay clattered into the courtyard, scattering sheep, Artemis at its heels—stopping near the house, which stood empty to Val's insistent knock.

"In here," Penny called from the lambing barn, where she, her father, and two of the shepherds stood ankle deep in straw, their hands bloodied by sheep that lambed early, sheep that bleated with such mutual discomfort she must concentrate all of her empathy and energies in trying to save those she could, lest she fall into an ineffectual despair of weeping.

He strode across the farmyard, not at all the figure she had hoped to see. Not Val she longed for—Val, who threatened Felicity's well-being, Val, who had wedged himself and his evil intent between her and the man she had given her heart to. She steeled herself against this fresh intrusion. She had no time for a wastrel today.

"I found this in the bottom of the watering trough."

One of the shepherds knelt beside her, beside the struggling ewe she thought to lose within the hour if it followed the pattern of the last. In his hand a soggy bit of browned plant, a distinctive seed pod still clinging to its leggy stem.

"Larkspur!" she cried. "Dear God, nary a wonder why they are all lambing at once. We shall be lucky if they live."

Val's lanky bulk darkened the doorway. "She is ill."

"They are all ill, and you stand in my light," she said, no more than a glance in his direction, wishing him gone.

"They sent her home fevered and coughing," he said.

A chill ran down her spine, raising the hair at the base of her neck. She looked up from the suffering face of the sheep, at a Val more haggard than when last she had seen him—great dark circles under his eyes, his hair badly in need of a clipping. A somber and humbled Val.

"Felicity?" She rose at once, wiping her hands on her apron, the ewe rising as well, her plaintive bleat voicing Penny's inner anxiety.

He nodded. "Yes. She asks for you. Will you come?"

She was shocked into silence. Things must be dire indeed if he came to her with such a request.

The ewe lumbered a few steps, then sank, too weak to go farther.

"Hollings," she said to the shepherd, "you must see to her. Tell my father I've business at Wharton."

Hollings nodded and made a grab for the ewe.

"Dr. Terrance?" She brushed straw from the apron, briskly loosing the strings.

"Come, and gone," Val assured her. They stepped through the doorway into the wind. He raked a hand through freshly tousled hair, his eyes closed, expression melancholy. "Dosed her with all manner of powders and pills. But she gets worse rather than better."

"Oh, dear. I will come at once. I have only to wash up and change clothes. Will you wait?"

"Yes." He sounded impatient and tired. "But not long. I do not like to leave her. Betty and Tess are next to useless when she frets."

"I will hurry."

He amazed her afresh in thinking to ask, "Shall I saddle a pony?"

"Please," she called out as she ran to the house. "The dark one."

Alexander watched them ride together from the farmyard, Penny and Val, the dog at their horses' heels—a pair so unexpected he stood flabbergasted in watching them go. And when they had rounded the bend, never looking up the rise where he stood, hoofbeats fading, he turned, crestfallen, his first thought to go back to the King's Head.

One last glance toward the farmyard, and he changed his mind, curiosity getting the better of him.

The lambing barn was a battlefield, utter chaos—ewes staggering about, bleating piteously; new lambs, still wet with afterbirth, struggling to rise. Dead sheep—they certainly looked dead—lay like piles of shorn wool amid bloody straw.

Alexander thought of the battlefield at Waterloo, of his nephew lying pale and still in his little coffin.

"Mr. Foster, sir?"

Penny's father failed to look up from the lamb he was wiping down with a bit of rag. "This one looks all right," he said.

"A fine little fellow," Alexander agreed.

Bloodshot eyes turned his way in surprise. "Mr. Shelbourne! What do you do here?"

"I have come to speak to Penny."

The old man sighed, then waved a weary, blood-streaked hand. "Just missed her. Gone to Wharton to see the child, who is as ill as my sheep it would seem."

Alexander thought of his nephew tossing and turning, delirious with fever, tender as the newborn lamb, just as wobbly on his feet.

"Here's another one dead, sir," cried one of the shepherds.

"What is wrong with your sheep?" Alexander asked.

She tried to stay calm on the way to Wharton Manor, their gait a quick trot, too fast for conversation, and yet she longed to urge the pony to a gallop. Felicity was ill, poor darling, seriously so. She thought of Alexander Shelbourne's nephew, and as quickly shoved the idea of him from her head.

Not that ill.

Her heart raced. *Oh, Lord and Lady Anne, please not that ill.*

"Do you hate me?" Val asked as he held wide the door that had so long held her at bay. "I would not blame you if you did."

Penny paused, studying his face by clouded daylight, the face she had once loved, grown world-weary. "I find hate, anger, even regret a waste of energy, Val. Where is she?"

At her feet, leaning hard against her leg, Artemis watched and listened.

Val motioned toward the stairs, and without another word she hastened up them, the dog leaping up the risers ahead of her.

The ewe rolled her eyes and struggled a bit, but they managed to jam the funnel in her mouth and poured in as much milk as she would swallow.

"You think this will work, do you?" Mr. Foster asked skeptically.

"The company physician used it on one of my men when poison was suspected. He said it doesn't always work. I've no idea how sheep will respond."

"Well, it's something, lad. Better than simply watching them die. Do you mind going about with your funnel, seeing to the worst of them?"

"Not at all, sir. I only hope it helps more than it hurts them."

The sheep vomited, as he had hoped. Mr. Foster nodded his approval.

"Good lad," he said warmly. "Your assistance is greatly appreciated."

Penny opened the door to the darkened nursery. Artemis paused on the threshold, growling low. For a moment Penny thought of the chaos of the lambing barn, of the dreadful trouble she had abandoned her father to. The nursery had something of the same odor, and dear Felicity, poor lamb, sat propped in a tumbled bed, sniffling, watery-eyed, her hair a tangled cloud around her highly flushed face, teeth clenched against the spoon one of the maids tried to force.

"Artemis!" the child cried weakly. The dog raced to her at once, growl deepening as she neared the maid, her defensive posture a wonder to behold.

"Artie, lie down," Penny chided as the woman froze with fear, spilling medicine, a blotch of brown on Felicity's rumpled white bedclothes.

"Penny!" Felicity's features brightened briefly before she glanced down at the stain and burst into tears.

"Dearest, hush now," Penny crooned as she enfolded Felicity in her arms and waved away maid and spoon.

"But she must take her medicine." The maid fretted almost as much as the child.

Penny nodded as she loosed her hand gently from Felicity's hot clutch and slipped the ribbons on her bonnet.

"Of course she must, as soon as she is calmer and the room set to rights. It smells as if the chamber pot needs to be removed. The bedclothes have now to be changed, and a warming pan must be brought up. Will you be so good as to send for the housekeeper? I require a bowl of broth, some calf's jelly and tea, with honey and a lemon if they are available."

"The housekeeper is gone, miss, but Betsy will fetch them, if you please." The girl set down bottle and spoon and hurried to the bellpull.

Penny wrapped Felicity in her shawl, and going to the window, opened it a little for fresh air. Then she took Felicity in her arms and cradling her fever-sweated brow against her breast, sat in the rocking chair and crooned nursery songs. When Betsy brought the tray, amidst the bustle of the bed being cased in fresh linens, she spooned a little broth into Felicity's mouth, and when she coughed, encouraged her to drink weak tea with honey and lemon.

Felicity soon dropped off to sleep in her lap, and as Betsy came to take away the tray, Penny asked, "When is the housekeeper expected to return?"

Her question met with silence and an uneasy exchange of glances between the maids, and then Artemis lifted her head to stare past them, and Val spoke, detaching himself from the shadows at the doorway. "I scared her away."

Penny rose, the child in her arms, and as she tucked her snugly into the bed, the dog like a shadow, always at her side, Val crossed the room, murmuring, "You are very good with her. I should have called for you at once."

Artemis made another low rumbling noise. Penny bade her be still, though in truth she was as uneasy as the dog with Val's presence, with his compliments. "How did you scare your housekeeper away?" she asked.

"Come," he said, his voice low. "We will wake her."

The level of his concern for the child surprised her. She followed him downstairs, Artemis padding at her heels. Supper awaited them in chafing dishes in the dining room, with three of the staff ready to serve them, even Artemis to be accommodated. One of the footmen lured her to the kitchen with meat scraps and the promise of a bone.

When the soup had been served, Val answered her question.

"Mrs. Olive," he began, and when she looked at him, brows raised, he clarified, "the housekeeper, did not care for drunkenness. Two of the downstairs maids, my valet, and a footman, have also lately left Wharton, vowing never to return." He slurped a spoonful from his steaming bowl. "Mother will be miffed. She liked Olive."

Penny noticed that the soup was served with only water to drink, that the second course arrived with syllabub, no wine to be seen. The decanters on the sideboard stood empty.

Val looked up from buttering his bread and noticed the direction of her gaze. "I have thrown it all away," he explained. "Every drop of it, save what my father keeps in the wine cellar."

"You surprise me," she said, the soup rendered tasteless by shock.

"Yarrow has the only key." He blurted the words, as if anxious to further impress her with the seriousness of his intent. "I have instructed him not to give it to me, no matter how piteously I beg, no matter if I threaten his job. I would stop this madness, you see. Put an end to it."

"Good," she said. "Very good, Val."

His gaze locked on hers a moment, as if her praise moved him, as if he were incredibly hungry for approval, and then he looked away. The moment passed, and she wondered if she had imagined the change in his features, the wolfish need. The rest of the meal slipped by in small talk, and as a fruit compote and strong, hot coffee were served with a wheel of white cheese, she smiled and said, "And now I must check on Felicity again before riding home. Do you mind if I return in the morning?"

"Stay the night," he said, and for a moment the look returned to his eyes. "I will have a room prepared."

She looked uncertainly at her spoon. "I . . . I do not think . . ."

"We will send word to your father."

The troubled blue of his eyes startled her. He wore the look of a man tossed by an unruly sea, who gazed upon his only anchor.

Artemis, who had slipped into the dining room as dessert was served, rose from her spot at Penny's feet, a high-pitched whine leaking from her throat.

Penny rose as well, shaking her head decisively. "Unless she is worse, you can well manage on your own. Father needs me. Besides, it will be best if she learns to rely on you for comfort."

He looked surprised, a trifle panicked. "But . . ."

She smiled and took his hand. "You do well by her, Val. I am glad of it."

"Penny." He followed her, reaching for the door that he might open it. As she passed, he grasped her hand, and despite Artemis's growl, stared deep into her eyes, reminding her of the way he had once looked at her long ago. The clock in the corridor chimed. He looked down and let go her hand. "I am sorry . . . about Eve . . . about everything. I should never have taken her from you."

She gave his arm a brief squeeze, and thinking of Alexander and the dreaded accusation of self-sacrifice, replied, "Perhaps it is best, after all. She ought to know her father."

He laughed, then closed the door to the dining room behind them, shutting off the light and warmth of the fire. In the sudden darkness, he said with bitter sarcasm, "He is a fine fellow—when not in his cups."

She found the farm much quieter than when she had left it. The lambing barn gave off a horrible stink, but the sheep had settled for the night, new lambs huddled close for warmth.

Her father and two of the shepherds sat hunched over cups of tea in the kitchen, trenchers of bread and cheese fast being reduced to crumbs among them.

"I am sorry not to have returned in time to fix you something hot," she said as she went in, pulling the bonnet from her head, pouring a cup of tea to join them.

"How is she?" her father asked.

"Feverish. Coughing. Settled for the night. I go back in the morning. How is the flock?"

The shepherds avoided her eyes.

Her father sighed. "Five dead. Some of the lambs too early, not likely to survive, but we might have lost more had it not been for that nice Mr. Shelbourne of yours."

Not hers anymore. Had he ever been?

"Mr. Shelbourne was here?" She dropped a lump of sugar into her tea.

"Aye. Came looking for you." Her father leaned back with a yawn, stretching his back until it made a crackling sound. "To wish you farewell."

She flinched, her spoon clinking the side of the cup. "He is leaving?"

"Aye. In a few days, he said. Kindly lent a hand."

In a few days? Could she bear it?

"A canny one, that," Hollings said. "Who would have thought to give them milk?"

Her father nodded. "May have saved half the flock. We owe him dearly, lass."

The following morning came too soon, on the heels of a restless night, and Penny made a point of riding through the village on her way to Wharton Manor. She did so that she might purchase horehound drops and an elixer of hyssop from the local apothecary. As she passed the King's Head, she found herself looking for Alexander Shelbourne, hoping for, and yet dreading an encounter. She must thank him for what he had done. She must tell him he had been right about Val.

She did not see him, indeed she had given up hope of it and was passing over the old wooden bridge, her mind now fixed on Felicity and how the poor little dear might have passed the night, when a man called out, "Miss Foster!"

Her heart lurched. For a moment she imagined it must be him, but the voice was wrong, not Alexander but Oscar scrambled up from the riverbank, fishing pole in hand, his hat bristling with feathery hooks.

"How do you do, Miss Foster?"

"My father's flock suffers, but I am fine," she said.

"I had heard," he said, "from Cupid that the child was sent home ill." He wore a worried look, and for that she silently blessed him. "How does she?"

"I am on my way to sit with her now."

"Valentine relents then, and allows you to see her?"

"He does. He is, in fact, a changed man."

"Val? How so?"

"He has stopped drinking."

"Sober, is he? I should like to see that."

"Do you care to come with me then—to pay your respects?"

"Ah, not at the moment. Rather bad timing, you see." He waved his pole. "The trout are biting, and I smell rather fishy. I do believe we have rain on the way. But the child? No chance she will end up—like Cupid's nephew, is there? He would never forgive himself."

She sighed. "He ought not burden himself with even the beginnings of guilt. Will you tell him that? He could not have gotten her here any faster. She was on her way home when Val . . ." She sighed. "At the time of the shooting match."

He nodded. "He will be glad to hear of it. Walks the fells, he does. Every day. Paces the room like a man possessed. No patience for fishing. Seems a bit melancholy since the wedding."

And she the reason, she thought, her tongue cleaving to the top of her mouth.

"You know we leave in three days?" he asked.

"Do you?" As her father had said, then, it is true. She felt them lost to her already.

Oscar ran a finger along the ridges in his cane pole. "I know it is most forward of me to ask, but do you mean to speak to him?"

She said nothing for a moment, then took a deep breath and said, "Yes, of course. I must thank Mr. Shelbourne for what he did yesterday for my father and the flock."

"He did it for you, you know. Loves you, he does. Do you love him?" he asked flatly, catching her off guard.

She threw her head back, one hand clutching the

brown paper parcel from the apothecary's, the other covering her mouth, the mouth he had kissed, oh, so long ago. She mumbled, "I am not certain he still loves me."

"Ha. Surely you jest. I have never seen him so besotted."

She frowned. "But, perhaps he has told you . . . I asked something of him I should not have."

"Enough that he could not forgive you for it?" Oscar lost hold of his line, the hooked end swinging in her direction like the pendulum in a clock.

"I am very much afraid so." Nimbly, she grabbed the line and handed it back to him.

He clasped it more carefully to the pole, saying, "You could go to him now. He was asleep when I left, but must be up by now."

She imagined him in bed, eyes closed, face gone soft with sleep, as he had been after his fall from Nichol's chair. "I cannot. Felicity . . ."

"Needs you?" He finished the thought.

Did she imagine it, or was there the faintest trace of derision in the way he said the words?

As she rode away, all she could think of was the sin of which Alexander Shelbourne had condemned her—self-sacrifice.

The morning found Felicity fretting and feverish with a rasping cough and watery eyes. An exhausted Val rocked her in his arms, gently trying to coax her into taking a drink of milky liquid.

"If you will swallow it like a good girl, Felicity, my love, I will give you horehound drops to suck away the bad taste," Penny said from the doorway.

Val looked up with a sigh of relief, and in his face she saw the boy he had once been. "I began to think you did not mean to come," he said, and in his voice she heard the boy he still was.

"As I promised," she said. "But you do quite well without me."

"Do not say so," he groaned. "I have been up all night."

Indeed, he did look tired.

"Well, now I have come, you must rest," she said.

He seemed happy to oblige, and went away as soon as Felicity had taken her medicine.

It rained all afternoon, a great, noisy, soaking deluge that turned the already muddy roads into an impassable morass. Penny stood in the window at Wharton Manor, listening to Felicity's ragged breathing, listening to the wind drive sheets of rain against the windowpane, and wondered if Alexander Shelbourne might postpone his leaving. She hoped he would.

She had nursed her hurt, her belief that he was wrong, and she was right. She had held it close to her, waiting for him to call on her, to apologize. She knew now, on this rain-drenched afternoon, that he would not call, that he was not in any way to blame for the child who murmured uneasily in the bed behind her.

She must set things right between them.

It had taken years of individual actions—hers, Val's, Eve's—for the child to end up here, prostrate and ill. She knew, in a way, that this illness was in some way a gift from God to Val, that he might rise above his weaknesses and strive to be a whole man.

Not a drop had he drunk since she had come to care for Felicity. Haggard and sunken-eyed he might be, but he was sober, anxious to help in Felicity's care, humble in accepting Penny's assistance.

And as much as she wanted to be indispensible to him, to Felicity, she knew deep within that it was best if they were not so completely dependent upon her, best that she trust in him. If he would carry the burden of responsibility, she must allow him to do so. Felicity was his daughter, after all, and it was clear from the way he tended her, from the way he had written down the visiting physician's every suggestion, that he meant to do his best.

And so, she set off down the stairs at the noon hour, ready to ride again to Appleby, thinking as she went of Alexander Shelbourne, of all that she must say to him, of how she would beg him to believe in her again, to refuse to let her go.

It was with complete astonishment she met Yarrow's response to her question, "Is your master better rested now?"

"I hardly think so, miss. It is difficult to rest, horseback."

"I do not understand."

"Rode away, miss. Right after your arrival."

"Gone?" she said in disbelief. "Where?"

Yarrow stared blankly at the wall. "His lordship did not see fit to inform me, miss."

It still rained as daylight faded. What had been a gentle mist became a peltering assault with the coming darkness, thunder rumbling, lightning a momentary brightness.

Alexander shared a dinner of the latest catch with Oscar at the King's Head—fresh trout, sauteed in butter and dill. The pale flesh fell from the bones, flakey and moist, as easily as his life seemed to fall apart, Alexander thought, nothing left to hold it together.

He agreed to Oscar's suggestion of a game of darts afterward in the pub. "But first," he said, "I would check on the gray."

"And a quick trot out to the Foster farm to ask after the flock?" Oscar suggested with a wink.

Alexander shrugged, unable to smile. "Just a quick walk down Bridge Street to clear the smoke from my lungs, and to check on the gray," he insisted.

Appleby hunkered down in the rain, gutters running full, the sight of other people's lives framed golden in lamplit windows. How he had longed for such light and crackling fires and a full belly on many a march. How easy, he thought, to step inside and forget. It was only in standing outside, dripping wet, looking in, that the memories flooded back—memories he ought not forget. Must not. Must not grow complacent—to the bounty that was his.

Oscar's suggestion that he ought to ride out to the Fosters', to ask after the state of the flock, to encounter, God willing, one more time, Penny Foster seemed part of that bounty he ought not take for granted, ought not let slip from his grasp.

As Val had.

And yet, it would seem he was to have one more chance with Val—one more encounter.

It was in the stables, as he wiped the wet from his face, he set eyes first on Val's horse, then Val himself, as he staggered in out of the rain, bellowing for his bay to be saddled, "At once!"

Too familiar that tone in his voice, the drunken weave of his gait.

"Stand still," Val admonished the beast gruffly when it was held for him, and he could not see fit to put foot to stirrup.

"So, Val!" Alexander stepped from the shadows. "Miss Foster's glowing reports of your transformation were premature."

Val swung his head heavily, raindrops flying from drenched locks as he settled in the saddle. He blinked a moment without recognition. "Pox on the woman," he drawled. "Pox on you, as well, Cupid."

Alexander frowned. "And the child?"

Val laughed, rubbing his nose dry on dripping sleeve. "Had you not heard?" he asked. "Brought a pox home with her, little vixen." He turned the horse toward the rain-curtained doorway.

Alexander called after him. "You cannot go on like this, Val. Must not."

Val stopped the horse with a wrench on the reins, and without turning said, "Could not go on listening to the voices, Cupid."

"Voices?" Alexander breathed in disbelief. He knew what voices, and yet this was the first time he had heard mention of them from Val, whom he had believed impervious to bad memories.

Val spoke to the flashing curtain of rain. "Do not pretend you never hear them."

"I hear them," Alexander admitted. "In the wind, and yesterday at Foster's farm."

Val turned at that, eyes gleaming. "Yes. The cry of the lambs."

A moment of grim silence hung between them, the horses shuffling in their stalls, the ostler's lad staring at them wide-eyed, still holding the door wide for Val. The warm smell of hay and dung and musky rain enfolded them, safe for the moment, from the wet rumble of thunder.

"Mercy," Val murmured, shifting in the saddle, leaning low that he might clear the doorway, digging home his spurs. The bay leapt into violent motion through the curtain of rain and into the night as Val said savagely, "And we showed them none."

Chapter Twenty-three

Sadly, Alexander rode into the bleakest of nights, not to follow Val, not to try to resurrect a friendship that withered on the vine, but to visit the Foster farm one last time, that he might see how the flock did, that he might wish Penny farewell.

Disappointment met him when he arrived to find her gone.

"Tending the child again," her father said. "But, don't stand there in the wet. Come in. Come in." He swung the door wide in welcome.

Alexander almost tripped on entering. The threshold required picking one's feet up, while the dated lintel hung so low he was forced to crouch. A hall ran from the front to the back of the place, floored in pebbles, the right-hand wattle-and-daub wall stacked with sacks of grain, a shelf running above from which a number of tools dangled.

They passed an open doorway, horseshoes nailed above, stacks of firewood upon one wall within, and shelves of pickled and potted goods, a baking stone, and rows of grain casks. *Her pickled goods. Her baking stone.*

Passing through a stone arch and up two steps into the other half of the building, it being slightly higher on the incline, they passed a stone stairwell that whistled a bit in the wind. *Cold. Did she sleep in the cold?*

Bedchambers above, Alexander knew. He had been offered a chance to recover from his fall in one of those bedchambers. She had sat beside him, bathing his forehead with vinegar. She had wanted him to stay.

Did she want him still? Did she want him enough?

They entered the warmth of the main rooms where a peat fire burned low in a great, hooded fireplace. The floors were slate, mullioned windows offered a dim light, supplemented with rushes, and two barley twist candles upon the great oak table.

It was a cozy place, neatly arranged, everything tidy. She had made it so.

Could he be happy here? He might fit the whole of it into his father's stable. The furnishings were heavy oak, elaborately carved. A settle by the fire, a spice cabinet built into the wall, dated 1674, a cupboard so large it served as a wall, a case clock that ticked away the moments.

He felt instantly at home.

They warmed themselves by the fire over cups of hot coffee.

"She will likely be late again, like last night," her father said. "Came in an hour or more after you had left us. Let me thank you again for that. Up with the roosters this morning, Penny was."

"And how does Felicity do?" Alexander asked, as he rubbed down his head with a bit of linen. The toweling smelled of lavender, like Penny. Alexander buried his nose in it as he dried his forehead.

The old man shook his head. "Feverish. She said the child had bumps. Contagious, she feared, and yet she is not convinced it is smallpox."

"What then?"

Her father shrugged. "I only know she asked me to keep my distance until she was certain she had not contracted the illness."

"And the flock, sir?"

"Ah. Kind of you to ask, lad." He said it with shaken head and a drawn-out sigh. "Seven dead, including the lambs, a half dozen more very shaky on their pins, and yet I think we are over the worst of it if the newborns do not catch chill from this dreadful downpour." He went to the window and peered out. "I will be that glad when Penny finds herself a husband to help with the flock on wet evenings like this. I've a touch of the rheumatism, you see."

Alexander nodded. "My father suffers too, when the wind blows from the northwest."

Mr. Foster tossed the dregs of his coffee on the fire. "It is a dreadful thing, this getting older, lad. Tell me, do you still mean to avoid growing a day or so older here in Appleby? Will you be leaving us if the roads are knee-deep in mud?"

Alexander thought about it a moment, the smell of whiskied coffee warm against his nose, the patter of the rain threatening an uncomfortable ride back to the inn. "I've nothing to keep me here," he said. "And decisions to be made about a future outside the military. I would not be dependent upon my father's largess, you see."

The old man laughed dryly. "And here I was thinking you might be dreaming of depending upon mine."

Alexander squinted at him over the brim of his cup.

Mr. Foster smiled. "I could just see you making my girl happy, perhaps giving her a wee one of her own, so she need not mourn Felicity's going."

Alexander cleared his throat. "I had at one time just such a picture in my own head."

"No longer?" the old man's brow furrowed.

Alexander felt he owed Penny's father the truth. "I fear she loves the child more than she loves me, sir."

"No, lad." His voice carried the amusement of a father who thought he knew all there was to know about his child.

Alexander knew it an unmerited confidence. "We had words," he said. "She made her priorities clear."

"Are you sure, lad? That is not at all the sense of

it I have from her. Will you not go to Wharton and speak to her?"

Alexander rubbed his brow and stood. "I am unwelcome there. You will tell her I called? That I shall try to call again before I go?"

"Aye, lad. I'll tell her right enough. She'll be sorry to have missed you."

"I hope you may be right in that."

Mr. Foster walked him to the door, and as Alexander donned his hat, he said, "I would not be one to stand in your way, son, if you see fit to change your mind and hers."

Warmed by the words, Alexander looked him in the eyes, clapped him briskly on the shoulder, and stepped into the spattering mist.

The rain continued, damp and dismal and unending, and Penny, unwilling to leave Felicity alone in the care of the maids, sat at the window and waited for Val's return by the clouded light of the moon.

She fell asleep before he galloped home again, her cheek cradled in her arm, face pressed to the cold pane. Her back was bent into a most uncomfortable position when she woke to words from the maid. "The master has returned—in the wee hours."

She was on her way downstairs to give him a piece of her mind when Felicity roused, begging for a drink. The child's forehead felt cooler. Her color seemed less elevated. She suffered nothing but the trace of a cough, and a rash of worrisome white bumps behind her ears.

"May I get up?" Felicity wanted to know, and Penny said she saw no reason to keep her confined.

"You may play quietly with your dolls," she said as she gazed out of the window in the direction of Appleby, looking for a man, as she had the night before. Not Val, of course. She had but to walk downstairs to find Val.

"Do not let me catch you running about without slippers on your feet," she said absently, turning from the sight of an empty road.

When Felicity drank broth with greedy enthusiasm and asked if she might have toast cut in fingers to dunk in it, Penny believed the worst was over. With exhausted elation, she went to tell Val his daughter recovered.

She found him in the library, lounging in a wingback chair by the fire, a pistol in his lap, a glass in hand, and a decanter on the table beside him.

"Do I disturb you?" she asked curtly.

"Not unless you bring me bad news or lectures," he said with a negligent wave of the glass. "How fares Felicity?"

"Why do you not look in on her?"

"In this condition? I think not." He smiled sardonically, then downed the spirits in a single gulp.

She frowned, back and neck aching, in no mood to put up with his weaknesses. With a sigh, she crossed to the fire, stirred the white hot ashes, and put on another log. "I thought you wanted to stop drinking."

"Changed my mind."

"Can you not change it back again?" She turned at the clink of crystal to find him holding the decanter. "Is not every swallow a choice?"

"To drink, or not to drink? Is that the question?" He laughed, the laugh ending in a cough, and with shaking hand allowed the amber liquid to splash into the glass. "I thought you came to discuss my daughter's health."

"I do, and your drinking affects it."

"Did she, too, wake with a headache, a burning thirst, and little desire to go on living?"

She shook her head. "I am in no mood for banter, Val. She recovers. Her fever is gone. No thanks to you."

"Splendid. I have not killed her after all." He threw back half the drink with a wince.

"As well you might have, leaving her as you did last night. Not bothering to come home. Did you simply assume that I would stay and care for her while you went away and got foolish?"

He lifted the glass to her. "Did you not do just that? You become too predictable, my dear. It never crossed my mind that you would not do what was best for the child." He yawned. "Even if it came to the compromising of your good name in staying here overnight."

He swallowed more spirits and said sarcastically, "Ah, but you have already given away your character for her sake, haven't you? So you'd nothing to lose."

Head aching, she turned her back on him in disgust, Alexander Shelbourne's accusation ringing in her ears. *Self-sacrifice.* Did she give herself away completely?

"I leave now, Val," she said flatly, longing for home, for sleep, for a quieting of the pounding in her head. "I entrust Felicity to you."

And as she walked away from him, she heard him laugh, and the clink of the decanter again as he said dryly, "She must be well if you would leave her to my care, my dear."

Alexander rode through the rain to Val's this time, sure he would find Penny there.

Yarrow met him at the door with the news. "I'm sorry, sir. Miss Foster left us about three quarters of an hour ago."

"So early in the morning?" That struck him as odd. "Miss Felicity is not . . ." He left the idea unspoken. He could not bear to think that another child was dead.

"Much better today," Yarrow said.

Alexander let free the breath he had not even realized he was holding. "And has her complaint been identified?"

"I do not think it has, sir. Though I daresay it is not smallpox, as she has no visible eruptions."

"May I see her?"

"Best not, sir. There is still some fear of contagion."

"And Val? Will he accept a call?"

"Do you mind waiting here, sir? I shall just go and see if he is at home to visitors."

Alexander did not enjoy the wait, though he was, for the moment, out of the wet. He would much rather be drenched and on the road after Penny than kicking his heels in Val's Great Hall.

He half expected Yarrow to return with a refusal, half hoped as much, but such was not to be the case.

"This way, sir," the aging butler said, and led the way past the family portraits in the stairwell and into the drawing room with its blazing fire and fogged windows.

A click met their entrance, a click that made Alexander's nerves jump. Too well he knew that sound.

Yarrow did not so much as glance at the blue-barreled hunting pistol Val had trained on him as he held wide the door and announced, "Mr. Shelbourne, sir."

Val made no effort to rise from the chair where he sat, gun in one hand, glass in the other, saying only, "Open a window, will you, Yarrow? And damp down the fire. It is too bloody warm in here."

The room felt cool enough to Alexander, but perhaps he was chilled by the sight of a pistol in Val's shaking hands. Certainly Val looked hot, in no condition to be holding a gun, much less aiming it at his butler. Beads of sweat dotting his upper lip, he nonchalantly followed Yarrow's progress, the gun barrel like a pointer.

"Is the gun loaded, Val?" Alexander asked, deliberately keeping his tone mild.

"Shall we find out?" Val asked, turning the gun in his hand, pressing the barrel to his own temple.

"Yarrow will have a great bloody mess to clean up if it is." Alexander yawned.

"Indeed." Val laughed as he squeezed the trigger, the pin clicking on an empty chamber. "Lucky for Yarrow," he said with acid humor.

Alexander decided the room was very warm indeed as he allowed himself to breathe again.

Yarrow quietly left the room. Val nested the weapon in a velvet-lined case on the table beside him, then stripped away his loosened neck cloth and unbuttoned the top of his shirt. "Hotter than Hades in here," he said irritably.

"I've come to say farewell, Val," Alexander said, his eyes still on the pistol case. "I leave tomorrow."

"In this rain?" Val flung the neck cloth at him, an ineffectual assault. It dropped to the Turkish carpet like a downed dove. "You'll not go five miles. Can't fool me, Cupid," he said. "It's the girl you came after." The eyes he turned on Alexander as he rose were bloodshot, the lids at half mast. "She spent the night here, you know?" He shut the lid on the gun box with a bang.

"Because of the child?" Alexander surmised.

Val laughed and staggered to the open window. "No. Because of me."

Alexander frowned. "Because you were drinking, and she dared not leave the child in your care?"

Val grunted and pressed his forehead to the fogged pane. "And so, you leave, and leave her to plague me, do you?"

"You prefer to drink yourself to death without anyone's protest?"

"Exactly." Val slid down the window frame, carefully to begin with, falling the last little way with a thump, as if he misgauged the distance. He leaned his head over the rain-spattered sill, lifting his face to the wet, head tilted so that the rain drenched his hair and face.

He raked his hand through unwashed locks, ensuring they were sodden all the way to the nape of his neck.

Inwardly, Alexander longed to yank Val from the floor, to shake some sense into him, to beg him not to squander his life. But he knew Val would not listen. He had never listened in the past.

"Why do you choose to live like this?" he asked sadly.

Val withdrew from the window with a sudden upward stagger, flinging raindrops as he turned, clinging to the draperies for balance. "You really should take Miss Foster with you when you go." He wiped the wet from an angry face with the back of his sleeve. "The two of you were made for each other. You speak from the same mouth."

"I've nowhere to take her, Val."

Val lurched to the sideboard, grabbed up a decanter, and took a sloppy swig. "Oh, do not cry poverty, Cupid—stupid Cupid. I weary of it. Weary of it all. Don't suppose you'll stay and drink with me?" He held forth the decanter.

"No, thank you," Alexander murmured.

"Suspected as much." He sighed in one instant, bellowing for Yarrow in the next.

The door to the drawing room flew open with a polite "Yes, sir?"

"Show my guest to the door. He is just leaving."

Alexander regarded the remains of his friend with regret. "God be with you, Val."

"And to the devil with you," Val grunted.

Alexander shook his head sadly. "No, Val. It is you who goes to the devil by way of the bottle. My brave and valiant friend, do not tell me you saved my life only to throw away your own."

"I begin to think I should have let you die," Val retorted.

Alexander laughed as he walked out the door, saying, "I would have haunted you, you know. Day and night."

Val had no answer to that, no ready retort.

As Alexander shrugged on his coat with the old man's assistance, he asked, "How long has he been like this?"

"Since she left, sir," Yarrow said evenly.

Alexander donned his hat. "Who sits with the child?"

"Betsy or Sue, sir. Sensible girls." Yarrow's face exhibited calm but for the pinched quality of his lips. "He shows no interest in her when he is in such a state, sir."

Alexander thrust on his gloves. "And the ammunition for his gun?"

"Locked away, sir. I have the only key."

"Good man, Yarrow," he said.

"You are very kind, sir," Yarrow murmured as he opened the door.

"And more than a little worried," Alexander said to the sky as the door closed behind him.

"Felicity improves," Penny said enthusiastically when her father held wide the door and she ran in out of the rain.

"Bad night?" he asked, worry etched deep in the lines of his face. "I expected you, lass."

"Oh dear! I am sorry, Father. Val abandoned us, you see. I fell asleep waiting for him to return. He staggered home at last, three sheets to the wind, I am told, as the sun was rising. I left him this morning well on the way to being completely inebriated before tea time. I hated to leave Felicity with him, but I am thoroughly exhausted, having slept in the windowseat. I mean to fall into bed for at least an hour before riding into Appleby to ask the apothecary about some little bumps behind Felicity's ears."

"Are you not hungry, lass?" he asked. "There's soup on the hob."

"More tired than hungry, but some of your soup sounds like heaven. Come. Tell me how the sheep do, while I sup."

"Would you not rather hear what I've to say about your marksman, Mr. Shelbourne?"

She made no attempt to disguise her surprise. "Do tell," she said.

Chapter Twenty-four

"You've the worst sense of timing in the world, lad" were the words Mr. Foster met him with when he responded to his knock, for the third day in a row.

"She's not here?" Alexander guessed. "Do not tell me she has gone to Wharton, for I have just been there, and would have passed her on the road."

Mr. Foster snorted. "She's off to Appleby now."

"Is she?" It crossed Alexander's mind she might have gone to see him, to wish him well before his leaving.

"Gone to the apothecary." Her father spoiled the daydream. "Something about bumps on Felicity."

"Bumps? But they told me at Wharton she does well."

"Aye. Penny concurs. But still she worries. Says Val is in his cups."

"Nose first," Alexander agreed. "Any thought on how to stop him?"

"Ah, lad. A body must want to stop, in order to stop."

Alexander sighed. "If that is true, he is well on his way to killing himself."

"Sad, that. A slow sort of suicide," the old man said, his expression bleak as he looked out over the fells. "I tried to stop her, you know."

"Your wife, sir?" Alexander did not pretend to misunderstand.

"Yes." He nodded, and looking Alexander straight in the eyes, he said, "Penny must be loving you, lad, if she's after telling you the truth about that."

And love for you, sir, has kept her locked in lies, Alexander thought as he mounted the gray and splashed back onto the muddy road to Appleby.

Penny left the apothecary's a packet of fever powder in her pocket, a growing sense of panic in her heart. She had intended to go by the King's Head before returning to Wharton Manor. Now she did not know if she dared risk taking the time.

And yet, she could not let her Cupid go. Nor Oscar. Not without a word. And so, she turned hurried steps toward the posting house and asked, standing well back from the desk, that the gentlemen might be called down to speak to her. She was informed by William, the desk clerk, who eyed her distant stance with undisguised curiosity, that one of the gentlemen in question had gone out that morning and had yet to return. A lad was promptly sent up for the one remaining.

Penny went to the window that looked out onto the street, making a point of standing well away from any of the patrons or employees of the posting house.

Oscar came down, and before he could get too close, she asked him to stop where he was, explaining, "I have been exposed to contagion, possibly the German measles. I would not want to chance making you ill as well."

The desk clerk, who stood at the near end of the desk, pretending not to eavesdrop, stepped back in alarm. Oscar nodded and motioned her away from the window. "Do you care to step into the serving area?" he asked. "You must be chilled. We could order a pot of tea?"

She shook her head. "I cannot stay. If it is measles, Felicity's fevers are not yet finished, and she will eventually break out in a rash. Val was well on his way to getting drunk when I left this morning. I dare not leave her care to him. But I had to come and say good-bye to you and . . ." Her voice dropped a little in saying,". . . to Mr. Shelbourne."

"You have not seen him, then?"

"Where?"

"At Val's. He set off this morning for Wharton. Hoped to catch you there."

"Did he?"

"Yes. Cannot think what keeps him. He has been gone for hours."

"Perhaps he stayed to speak to Val. If so, he is himself exposed to the measles, and you must inform him as much. You will also inform him that I regret very much not having opportunity to wish him well?" She turned to go.

"Miss Foster." He stopped her. "You do know it was not Val he went to see." Oscar plucked nervously at his mustache. "It is you he wants to speak to."

Alexander rode into Appleby, soaked to the skin, the rain fitting his mood. He went straight to the apothecary's, only to be told, as he had been told all morning, that he had just missed Miss Foster.

Defeated and chilled to the bone, he stepped from the shop, and taking up the gray's reins, turned toward the King's Head stables. As if to underscore his failure, the rain, which had been falling steadily, gave itself to greater vigor. With bowed head and deflated spirits, rain trickling uncomfortably down the back of his neck, he ran.

Ran straight into another running figure, head bowed against the deluge. He almost did not recognize her. Despite the dripping bonnet, that covered much of her head, her face was streaming wet and much bedraggled.

Penny Foster.

* * *

"Mr. Shelbourne," she said, her breath pluming in the cold, rain running like tears upon her cheeks, the signboard above the stable door banging in the wind. "I must ask you to stand well back from me."

He did not step back as she asked and did not relinquish his hold on her shoulder. "At last I find you, after searching all morning, and this is how you would welcome me?" His eyes gleamed with amusement beneath rain-beaded eyebrows. "It will not do, Penny. It really will not do."

He bent his head, as if to kiss her, right there in the middle of the street, where anyone might see them, and as much as she would have secretly loved him to do just that, she held him at arm's length, saying, "You must not. I fear contagion."

"Your warning comes too late," he said, undeterred.

"Are you ill, sir? Fevered?" She pulled off her glove that she might press her bare hand to his forehead.

He nodded, and indeed his forehead was warmer than her chilled fingers.

"Half sick with love," he said, taking her hand in his, turning it palm upward, that he might kiss away the raindrops. "Fevered with need."

She tried to free her hand, to push him away. "I would not make you ill, sir. Too much do I care for your well-being."

"Do you?" He smiled, his wet face unexpectedly beautiful as he slid his hand inside the cover of her cloak, seeking the warmth of her waist. "Ah, but you are the cure, my dear." He drew her closer. "Come. I would get you out of these wet clothes. I would warm you as you have never before been warmed."

"No," she said, her arms more forceful, though she was desperately in need of warming.

He silenced her with a kiss, lips trailing, kissing raindrops from her cheeks, lighting a fire with his breath, with the touch of flesh upon flesh, that coursed into the heart of her, and down, down, into the most private part of all that she was.

"I thought you had given up on me," he whispered, his voice husky. "That the child meant more to you than I."

"I am serious." She pulled away as he nuzzled her neck, warming her earlobe with his breath. "According to the apothecary, Felicity has—"

"The German measles," he said, both hands under cover of her cloak, encircling her waist, drawing her closer, a purposeful look in his eyes. "Had them when I was a lad."

At that, all the fight went out of her. She allowed him to kiss her forehead without complaint or resistance. She did, in fact, lean her head ever so briefly upon the solid comfort of his shoulder, sliding her cheek across the wet wool lapel of his coat, into the hollow of his neck. Breathing deep the wet, manly smell of him, wondering if her breath on his chin aroused him as much as he had aroused her, she said, "Will you come with me?"

"Where?" He leaned back, desire blazing in the depths of his eyes like fire, a conflagration that threatened to consume her.

"To Wharton," she said, and watched with regret the dimming of that brightness and warmth.

"I must let Val know Felicity has the measles. To expect the rash and the returned fever," she explained.

"Of course."

How crestfallen he looked, how cool his gaze as a pucker formed between his brows, as his hands left her waist.

"Val was in a bad way when I left him," he said, wiping the rain from his nose with the palm of his hand.

She shivered, suddenly chilled to the bone, hungry

for the return of his touch, for the heat in his eyes. "Drunk? Or ill?" she asked.

He frowned, all light and humor and love gone from his features. Worry traced lines in the corners of his mouth. His eyes looked more gray than green in the shadow of his hat brim. "Quite possibly both," he said.

Chapter Twenty-five

Together they set off in the miserable rain, as the clock tower above St. Lawrence's marked half past one, a lonely sound that echoed the feeling inside of him. Alexander was hungry for Penny Foster's affection. He was cold without her arms about him, and deeply concerned—for the child, for Val, and even more important—for the two of them. He had intended to kiss Penny Foster in the street, to tell her how much he loved her, to ask her to be his. He had begun to think the rain, and his failed attempts to find her, an omen of sorts, an indication that he was not meant to leave Appleby on the morrow after all. That he was to get on with the making of life rather than the taking of it.

And now that he had found her, had held her in his arms, and stood ready to offer her all that was left of him—once more, the child came between them. And while he could not in any way fault her for her concern—indeed, he joined her in worrying about poor little Felicity with Val as her protector—he was sure now he had been right in what he had told her father. She cared more for the child than for him. The truth of it was devastating.

She looked at him often as they rode. He could see the movement of her bonnet out of the corner of his eye, and yet he could not bring himself to look back at her, fearing she must see his pain, his hopelessness in the face of that which he had begun to hope for most.

He shivered in the cold, a cold that went all the way to the depths of him. He was reminded most vividly of other wet rides in the rain, of a similar sense of hopelessness, one he had hoped to banish in the warmth of his love for her.

He focused on the bobbing mane of the gray, up and down and up and down, and soon they would be there. He glanced at the rump of the pony, gone before his horse in the lane. It was the same pony's rump that he had seen that first day on the road into Appleby. A brown rump, grayed by the mist. He had asked her then if she needed his assistance, and she had refused him. Would she ever need him as he now needed her? He did not think so, and with that thought, he wondered, would he ever be warm again?

He had wanted to kiss her!

She could tell by the way he had looked at her that he had wanted to kiss her again, and hold her closer, and more, so much more. She had seen desire in other men's eyes, but never like this, never coupled with such warmth, such affection, such softness.

She blushed just to remember it, and all for her, and wondered if a matching desire glowed in her eyes as she glanced at the tall figure on the rain-drenched horse beside her. She could not deny she wanted what those heated looks had promised. She wanted his hands beneath her cloak—wanted all that she had once refused Val. She imagined him unbuttoning her bodice and peeling the cold, wet clothes from her back, that he might warm every inch of her with touches and kisses and the brush of bare flesh to bare flesh. Her breasts throbbed with need.

She wanted to lie with Alexander Shelbourne, to give of herself as she had never given before. She wondered if he knew, and flushed to think that he might, her cheeks heated and rain chilled at the same time.

She felt no embarrassment at all for her rain-bedraggled state. In his eyes she was beautiful, desirable—kissable. She even began to think he meant to offer the future she had despaired of—a future that included marriage, respectable connections, perhaps even children—a house full of children.

"Do you still mean to leave tomorrow?" she called out to him over the splashing thud of the horses' hooves as they turned into the avenue of trees that led to Wharton Manor.

He tipped back his head to answer, but a shout, much muted by the rain, interrupted his answer. A dark figure waved frantically from the hillside to their left, calling to them again. He was draped in a long cloak and overshadowed by a half-broken umbrella.

"Who is that?" Alexander asked.

"I do believe it is Yarrow." Penny frowned. "Though why he should be out in this dreadful downpour is beyond me."

Yarrow, not at all his orderly, austere self, drenched hair dripping into worried eyes, half walked, half slid down the slope, so great was his haste in approaching.

Out of breath, he leaned into the side of the gray, his pitiful umbrella dripping a curtain of rain. "He . . . he has taken her onto the fells," he said.

Felicity! Dear God, Felicity!

"Has he gone mad?" she demanded, rain dripping from her nose.

Yarrow nodded balefully. "A man possessed. Would not listen to a word of reason. Sent me after you, he did, when she grew feverish and refused her medicine. When I returned to tell him you were not to be found, he held her limp in his arms, covered head to toe in a red rash."

Penny gasped, terror gripping her heart, the cold and wet gripping her shoulders.

"Said he was entirely to blame. Said he were not fit to live with such guilt."

"Do not say she is dead," Penny begged with a shiver.

The old butler looked away uneasily, his mouth pursed. "I am afraid she may well be, miss. The maids tell me she was delirious, that he had to hold her down to force the quack's concoction. They were afraid to go near her—near him—when she went limp, miss."

"I should never have left them."

"And where are they now?" Alexander asked grimly.

Yarrow pointed up the hill. "Did not so much as stop to put on his cloak." He shook the sodden garment in his arms. "Just stepped out into the wet, left the door open, the rain peltering in."

"How long ago?"

"Cannot be far. On foot, he is."

"We must go," Penny said, kicking the pony into motion.

Alexander would have followed her at once. His hands had lifted the reins with that very end in mind, but another shout gave him pause, as a streak of black-and-white charged up the hill after Penny.

"So, it is you delays Penny in her errand," Mr. Foster said irritably, his nose very red beneath his dripping hat. "I began to worry about my girl when Wharton's man came asking after her, and she long since due at the Manor to my way of thinking."

"Perhaps it is best you are here with the dog, after all," Alexander leaned forward in the saddle. "Come, we've no time to waste."

Artemis led the way, and the three of them followed, the Fosters' fell ponies clambering up the hill with ease. Alexander's gray, being heavier and less familiar with the landscape, hesitated now and again, and slipped among the rocks.

The rain-laced sky, brooding, went from the dull gray of a dove's breast to the darker gray of the gun barrel protruding from Mr. Foster's saddle—a carbine, much like Alexander was used to shooting.

"Where are we going?" Foster shouted. "Would she visit her mother again in this dreadful weather?"

Alexander kept his eyes on the horizon, what little they might see in the eddies of the mist, and shouted back at him, "Her mother?"

The old man nodded grimly, rain bouncing from the brim of his hat. "The ravine," he yelled, "where she jumped."

Alexander goaded the gray to keep up with Foster's pony, the awful words resounding in his mind. "Let's hope that is not where he takes her," he said.

Foster turned to glare at him, confused. "He? Who?"

Ahead of them, Penny kicked her pony to greater speed.

"Val!" Her shout blew back at them. "Wait, Val!"

There they were, shadows in the mist ahead—a man staggering, something heavy in his arms, a pair of legs dangling, a bit of cloth fluttering in the wind.

Val turned his head ever so slightly, as if he heard Penny's cry, but his pace never slackened. He simply kept going, doggedly climbing the final slope to the ridge.

"We'll never get there in time," Mr. Foster shouted as he raised quirt to the winded pony. "The ravine is on the far side of that ridge."

Alexander reined the gray to a sudden standstill, his response instinctive. "Give me your gun," he said.

She kept riding, knowing she could never reach them in time, knowing Val was unstoppable, and yet she could not stop gigging the pony's ribs though the game little beast already went as fast as was prudent. She could not stop bruising his rump with the quirt, could not allow her world to step over the brink again—not again—without trying to halt disaster.

Thunder sounded behind her, and yet it was not thunder. A bee sang by her ear, and ahead of her Val staggered and tried to take another step, but his legs no longer worked right. He lurched, shifting the weight in his arms, falling to his knees with a howl.

The pony shook its head at the sound and slowed. She looked back as the truth of what had happened sank in. Her father stood holding the horse, his pony. Alexander rose from one knee, smoking gun in hand.

For a moment their eyes met. For a moment the significance of his action left her stunned—breathless. Had he killed Val? For her? For Felicity's sake? Had she driven him to this?

He dropped the gun, hands shaking, heart quaking, the sound of Val's cry of pain ringing in his ears. Instinct took over. He swung into the gray's saddle and sent the horse charging up the hill, his arms still vibrating from the blast of the gun, his mind in turmoil. Had he killed Val? Had he missed him and shot the child?

She rode on with an absence of feeling, a blankness of emotion, breath rasping in her ears, the pony winded as well. No race to get there now. She soothed the animal with a gentle word, perhaps with the hope of soothing herself—her voice uneven, her body beginning to shake.

Behind her, the thud of hoofbeats. Ahead, the dark, motionless lump that was Val, and Felicity, dear little Felicity. Too bleak a sight to regard for any length of time, and yet she moved toward it, inexorably, drawn and repelled, the rain suddenly too cold, shivers shaking her from head to toe—all of her cold except her eyes, her cheeks, which burned with tears as profuse as the raindrops dripping from her bonnet brim.

*   *   *

Did he move? Alexander wiped the rain from his eyes and focused again on the darkness that was Val.

He moved, definitely movement, not just the wind flapping wet fabric. Val not only moved, he writhed, and a moan arose from his throat like that of a wounded animal.

Alexander felt the pain of that cry all the way to his toes as he flung himself from the horse and knelt in the mud beside his injured friend.

Not dead—Val was not dead. *Thank God!* Shot through the fat of his calf, nothing vital, blood soaking his stocking, so very bright the color, alarmingly so.

"Lord!" Alexander breathed, his shoulders shaken by silent sobs of anguish.

Val turned on him, his face twisted with pain. Foul oaths cascaded like a river from his tongue. And yet, the hands that clung to the child were gentle. Felicity, dear little Felicity, lay curled in his arms—cradled—so small she looked, so pale and motionless, her lips a bluish tinge.

Penny slid from the saddle and went to them, limbs awkward, her breath catching in her throat, a cry rising like a bubble from deep within.

"Felicity, Felicity." The name spilled again and again from her mouth. *Not dead. Not dead.* She could not believe it was so. Would not. Sobbing openly, she knelt to stroke the dripping little head cradled against Val's chest.

So blue her lips, so pale her cheek.

"Cupid!" Val was shouting, spitting tears and rain and anguish, the movement of his chest making the sad little head bob. "Damn you. It hurts." He clutched at his leg, rocking with the pain. "Why not the heart, old friend? Why not that one last favor?" Val grabbed at Penny, blood staining her coat. "Where were you? She was burning. Burning. I didn't know what to do."

Penny fell back, stricken by the look in his eyes, by the bloody mess of his leg.

Alexander stripped off his neck cloth. "He may bleed to death yet if we do not get this tended to." He attempted to bind the wound, to hold the leg still.

"Stop!" Val tried to kick him aside, arms flailing, eyes bright, lips twisting as more tears coursed down his cheeks. "Let me bleed. Let me die."

"Hold him," Alexander ordered.

Penny obeyed, grasping the hands he flailed, pushing him back, Felicity still in his arms. "Good gracious!" she blurted. "He is hot." Her hand flew to his forehead. "Fevered."

"We must get him back to the Manor," her father said as he held still the injured leg.

Alexander swiftly bound the bloody wound, then lifted the child from Val's clinging grip, saying gently, "Let go, Val. Time to let her go."

He thrust the child into Penny's waiting arms. "Come," he said, looking Val in the eyes. "Here is your coat. You will ride my gray. See if you can stand."

Behind him, Penny bent over the child, murmuring. "Dear Lord! Dear Lord! We must get her in out of the cold." Her voice broke as she wrapped her cloak about the still form, so that they were both caped beneath the soggy wool. "We must get her to a doctor."

"The child's beyond caring about the cold, Penny, my dear," her father murmured as he assisted in the lifting of Val, who struggled against them in rising.

He needed her. They needed her to help calm Val, and yet she had eyes for none but the child. Clutching the still figure tight to her chest, she mounted her pony, oblivious to Alexander's voicing of her name, to her father's echoing cry.

Head bent over the bundle in her arms she goaded the pony into motion.

Chapter Twenty-six

They were met in the Manor yard by a half dozen of the servants, all ready and willing to help, to carry Val in, to take the horses, to tell them that Yarrow had sent for a physician. A hot bath had been prepared. The bedpan was warming. They must come in by the fire and dry themselves.

Val cried out in pain and anger as he was carried in.

Mr. Foster instructed anyone within hearing distance that young Wharton was ill as well as injured, that he must be handled with care.

"Yes," he was told. "Miss Foster said as much. She is upstairs, with Felicity."

Alexander slid wearily from the saddle, feeling much removed from it all—suddenly useless. He clung to the gray's reins when they would have led him away, insisting he would rub down the horse. The groom shrugged, then led Foster's pony into the warm hay and oats smell of the stables. He was given a rag, a brush, and a currycomb. He was left in a stall alone with the gelding, alone with shaking hands and an aching throat.

He rubbed down the gray, careful in the drying of ears and nose and fetlocks, checking the big hooves for stones, but beyond that he was not much use to the beast. He needed the gray more than the gray needed him. As he had after battle, he needed the comfort to be drawn from the great, warm size of the animal, from the unconditional acceptance to be found in his darkly intelligent eyes, from the whiffling noise of contentment made deep in his chest as he nosed at the bucket of oats.

Still wet, still cold, the ache in chest and throat like a weight of stones crushing him, Alexander bent his head into the gelding's steaming shoulder, and mouth wide, eyes streaming, shoulders shaking, wept—soundlessly. He could not allow the sobs to vent noise. He could not allow the groom to know.

Penny watched from the rocker by the fire, the child bundled in her arms. The bath she had ordered for Felicity was being prepared in all haste behind a folding screen. The whole household seemed anxious to help. Two maids waited for the pot of water to boil, two more ladled from the bucket of cold.

She listened to the commotion as Val was carried in, then rose to go to the window and saw her father follow, while Alexander Shelbourne turned his back on the house and led his horse away.

"The pot is steaming, miss!" one of the maids cried. There followed a great deal of splashing.

"You have warmed linen waiting?" she asked.

"Yes, miss."

Penny gazed down at the child, at the blue-tinged lips and eyelids. "Come, Felicity, my dear. A nice hot bath to warm you."

The maids stepped aside, heads lowered. She dropped the blankets and peeled the wet clothes from the limp, rash-covered body.

She plunged Felicity into the steaming water, mindless of wetting her sleeves or splashing her bodice.

"You must hold her head," she instructed one of the maids.

"Isn't it catching, miss?"

"Hold her head," she said again, firmly.

The woman knelt and did as she was bade.

Penny lifted the limp arms into the water, then took

the soap and lathered the body clean. She would not weep as she did it. She had no energy for weeping, only for the bathing of the body, for the prayers that ran endlessly through her mind.

There was a moment when she thought she saw Felicity's eyelashes flutter, when her heart lurched with hope, and as she lifted the body and wrapped it in warm linen and chafed the flesh dry, she said a little wildly, "How warm her skin. She looks as if she does but sleep. Are her lips less blue than before? Does she yet breathe? Bring me a mirror."

One of the maids hurried to comply, thrusting a hand mirror at her.

She held it to the child's lips, saw steam forming on the glassy surface, and almost cried out in her joy.

"Steam rises from the hot water, miss," Betsy pointed out gently, taking the mirror from her, the pity in her eyes unbearable.

"Can I do that for you, miss?" one of the maids asked.

Penny shook her head, wet locks dripping. "Leave me alone with her."

Penny sank once more into the rocker, Felicity bundled in blankets in her lap. *Lady Anne, Lady Anne. If ever I needed you it is now. Can you not have a word with God?* The fire crackled and sparked. Outside the wind blew. The water in the tub ceased steaming. The water cooled, motionless as the child.

"No," she said aloud. "No!"

Her father cleared his throat from the doorway behind her. He walked in, saying, "You must be getting out of those wet clothes, my dear, or you shall catch your death."

So much love in his voice. So gently did he insist, tears flooded her eyes. She could not look up at him. "I cannot let go of her now that she is in my arms, Father."

He nodded, the lines in his face etched deep, as he

drew another chair close to the fire. "Your mother said as much on the day you were born."

Penny turned to look at him. "But I did not think she wanted me."

"The day you were born, she could not have been happier. Would not let the wet nurse carry you away to feed. Insisted on doing it herself."

Penny was in tears again, the heat of them warming her cheeks, salt on her tongue, as they trickled in the corners of her mouth. "Did she? Did she, really?" Her arms wrapped tight around Felicity, sweet Felicity, wishing life into her again. *Lady Anne, Lady Anne. I cannot bear it.*

And from the depths of Penny's cloak came a small sigh, a sigh so lifelike she must stop weeping, afraid she squeezed the child's body too tight. She gazed down upon the unspoiled perfection of an unblemished cheek.

Eyelashes fluttered.

"Dear Lord!" Penny cried in disbelief. "A glass of water." She waved her hand at the pitcher, her eyes fixed on the miracle of Felicity's face as she stirred, groaning, color returning to her lips.

"You must tell Val," she said as he handed her the glass.

He nodded, dumbfounded, and made for the door.

"Penny?" Felicity whispered, opening her eyes.

Penny smiled and leaned in close to whisper, "Yes, my dear."

"I dreamed I was on fire, and Papa carried me into the rain."

"Hush now." Penny slid her beneath the warmed covers.

"And Papa?" Felicity tried to sit up.

"I will fetch him," Penny said.

Doctor Terrance entered.

Penny stepped aside, realizing she could not fetch Val, that he was in no condition to mount the stairs.

And yet, she must tell him Felicity asked for him. She must share her elation with . . .

Suddenly aware of who was missing from this moment, she raced for the door and down the stairs, standing aside for the passage of Val, who, despite his freshly bandaged injuries, insisted on being carried by two of the footmen to his daughter's bedside.

Her father followed. Their eyes met as Val was borne past her.

"Where is he?" she asked, the question urgent. "Do not tell me he has left."

Her father knew at once whom she meant. He frowned and said, "He may well have, my dear. I have not seen him since . . ."

She ran past him, grabbing up a dry cloak from the pegs by the door.

"He loves you, my dear," her father shouted after her. "But he thinks you care more for the child than . . ."

She heard no more as she ran into the rain again and across the carriage yard. The door to the stables opened with a squeal. The groom looked up from brushing down her father's pony. He seemed the only person there, but he tilted his head toward one of the stalls at her questioning look, and over the door she saw the twitch of gray ears.

"Alexander?" she said as she pushed into the stall.

His head, hair still sleek with rain, jerked up from the gray's shoulder, looking not at her, but away.

"Thank God, you are still here," she said.

"Why?" he said brusquely. "Why thank God? It is the devil who has been at work this evening." His voice cracked. He sniffed and wiped at his face with a damp sleeve, then bowed his head to the horse's flank.

The straw rustled against her skirts as she went to him, to place her hand upon his shoulder. He flinched at her touch.

Aware of how cold her wet shoes were, how bedraggled her hair, she cupped one hand against the gray's warm flank, reaching out once more with the other to touch his arm and said, "They both live."

His head came up at once. "What? I thought . . . I thought when you rode away without a word, that you had gone mad with grief."

She wiped a tear from her cheek. "The doctor is with her now, and Val"—she smiled—"Val has climbed the stairs, and the only thing I am wishing is that you . . . you will . . . please . . . not go."

He did not allow her to finish. Suddenly, she was wrapped in his arms, and his lips were warm on hers. The gray shifted position with a low whicker, pushing them closer still.

She warmed to him, to his touch, to the wonder of his mouth.

"I need you," she whispered against his lips. "It is you I will grieve for if you go. Hold me."

"I thought I had lost you," he murmured between kisses, his voice throaty. "I thought I had lost everything."

Epilogue

A four-day celebration was held for the June wedding of Miss Penny Foster to Alexander Shelbourne, affectionately known as Cupid by most of those who came. The wedding party was exceptionally large, encompassing most of the citizenry of Appleby, a large contingent of men in military uniform, a vast number of Mr. Shelbourne's relatives, including his father, Lord Shelbourne, and his two elder brothers and their wives.

Oscar served as best man, of course, and Fiona Greenlow as matron of honor. Little Felicity, fully recovered from her illness, strewed yellow rose petals and tiny purple and yellow touch-me-not blossoms before the bride as she walked down the aisle. Penny carried a bouquet of lily of the valley and lilacs. Transformed before the eyes of all, Penny was radiant with joy, her Valentine wish fulfilled in every imaginable way.

But the moment perhaps best remembered by all of those who witnessed the joyous celebration was the three-legged race. The prize, you see, was taken by Valentine Wharton, sober a full two months at that time, and his daughter, Felicity. Despite the disparity of the length of their legs, as well as the slight limp Valentine still suffered, the two hobbled across the finish line, laughing, arm in arm, declared the winners by all. It was later revealed, with a great deal of laughter, that the groom had quietly threatened to shoot anyone foolish enough to try to outrun the two.